RETURN

OF THE

SNOW GOOSE

A St. Elwood's Mystery

Diane Walker

978-1-304-29620-7

Dedicated with Gratitude

To the Shaw Islanders, who inspired me

To the SeaStars, who welcomed me

To the TeaTimers, who edited me and kept me sane

And to Chris, who loves me still in spite of it all…

CHAPTER 1

Hardly an auspicious beginning, thought Gemma as she tuned out the relentless drone of her new Senior Warden and absently watched the fog drift over the dock below her office window. She'd been thrilled when the bishop asked her to serve as interim vicar for the tiny stone church on Brandon's Rock. She was looking forward to a year in the islands, and the church was utterly charming, with a wonderful view of the bay and the Canadian mountains to the north. But on this cold November morning that view was swathed in gray mists, and the chill and damp were overpowering the ancient electric radiator that sat ticking ominously beside her desk.

Driving into town this morning from her cabin out at Neck Point, Gemma had passed a large white bird, perched squarely on the yellow line, as if it were sitting on a nest, its eyes wide open as a steady stream of pickups drove by -- mostly islanders on their way to construction jobs, with the obligatory black or yellow lab in the back, barking or wagging a tail in greeting to the other dogs in passing.

The bird, a snow goose, had obviously been stunned by a glancing blow from a car; crows were hovering nearby in anticipation of her inevitable end. Gemma felt tears spring to her eyes, seeing the trapped bird, and would have stopped to move it safely away from the road. But the trucks were speeding in a last-minute rush to the ferry, and she was already late for a 9:00 meeting, so instead she drove on and resolutely attempted to brush the image of the bird from her mind.

The warden, Mrs. Breezley, had already unlocked the church when Gemma arrived, and was standing in the tiny kitchen off the narthex glaring at the feeble microwave, in which she was warming a cup of what had to be yesterday's brew. "One of the first things you'll need to tackle, Mother Benson, is fund-raising. All those folks who left us over Father Parkinson's shenanigans? We need to get them back in the doors and contributing again. This kitchen is an outrage."

"Yes, Mrs. Breezley," Gemma had responded, reluctant to begin arguing this early in the morning. "but first – please, call mc Gemma?"

"I don't believe it sets the proper tone for the congregation, to address a priest – even if she IS a woman –" (said with a sniff) – "by her first name. I'm sure that's when things began to slide around here, when people started getting so familiar with Father Parkinson."

"Whatever," replied Gemma, unconsciously mimicking her younger daughter, Amy, now off to college on a soccer scholarship. "Shall we go to my office? I've turned on the heat; I'm sure it will be warmer there." Gemma glanced over at the coffee pot longingly, but clearly Mrs. Breezley had taken the last of the brew, as the glass pot sat empty beside the tarnished copper sink. She sighed and followed Marcia into her office, wishing there were some place to find a to-go cup filled with a hot Starbucks mocha breve.

The meeting was going predictably, thought Gemma, watching a seagull drop its shell on the dock outside her window. But it wasn't like the bishop hadn't warned her before she took the job.

When Sam Farwell, bishop of the Episcopal Diocese of Western Washington (and Gemma's former boss) had learned that Gemma's husband Alex had decided to go to India with Doctors Without Borders for a year, he'd called Gemma into his Seattle office. "Just a little chat," he'd said on the phone, but they both knew it would come to more than that. Her "little chats" with the bishop were almost always about troubled congregations, and this one was no different.

"I hear Alex is heading off to India again," he had said, with an inquisitive look. "Have you ever gotten over your aversion to our fair sub-continent?"

"Of course not," she shuddered. "Ugh. Heat, disease, poverty, dust and dung everywhere. I still don't understand why Alex loves it so."

Alex, a pediatrician, had fallen in love with India during their time together in the Peace Corps. He'd already gone back twice, doing month-long stints at a little hospital outside Kerala, on India's surprisingly Christian southern coast. But this time, now that both their daughters were off at college, he'd decided to follow a lifelong dream and stay there for the year.

"You could come, you know," he'd smiled, tenderly brushing her over-long bangs from her brow. "You know how much I'll miss you; a year is a very long time."

Gemma had smiled up at him. "I'll miss you, too, dear; you know that. But I'm not sure it's a great idea for all three of us to be out of the country when Amy's just starting college. What if something goes wrong, or she's miserable? Or what if Serena gets sick again in Taiwan and needs to come home?"

"You know that's just an excuse, don't you," sighed Alex. "If it were Venice you'd be there in a heartbeat." Hearing his name, Venice, their tuxedo cat, sauntered up and began a leisurely stretch up Gemma's pantleg. She leaned over and pulled him up into her arms before his claws could penetrate to her skin.

"Don't worry, old boy," she murmured into the cat's ear. "I'm not leaving; it's just Alex this time." Venice, named for the city Gemma loved so much that she'd visited it with each of their daughters, wrapped his forepaws trustingly around Gemma's neck and began licking her chin.

"I'm sorry Alex," she said again, gently disengaging from Venice's determined ministrations. "I'll miss you, too. But I got enough of India the first time around. I know you still have work to do there, but my job lies elsewhere. This will be good for both of us, to spend some time apart. After all, it's been almost 25 years."

"27, if you count all the time I spent on that couch in the dorm parlor waiting for you to get home from your dates with all those other guys," Alex grinned.

"Whatever," she smiled back, absently stroking the cat at her feet. "The point is, it's a chance for both of us to make a difference in the world in a way we couldn't when the girls were growing up. You know the bishop will have something juicy for me; the timing is too perfect for it to be otherwise."

Gemma had met Alex while attending seminary in Boston, where he was finishing up a medical internship. Though it may have been love at first sight for Alex, he would never have admitted it. And as for Gemma, she'd found his gruff manner too abrasive for her taste; for over a year after meeting him she had kept him at a distance, teasing him about his lack of a good bedside manner.

But over time their friendship had evolved, and they finally married the day before her graduation from divinity school, choosing for their honeymoon a two-year stint in India with the Peace Corps. Gemma had been ordained within a year after their return from India, and had just been called to her first pastoral position as an associate at a large Episcopal parish in one of Seattle's eastside suburbs when she learned she was pregnant with Serena.

Given that Gemma's due date coincided with the start of the school year and the congregation had been expecting her to head up their Sunday School and youth programs, Gemma had turned down the position and taken instead a part time job editing the diocesan newspaper. Eventually, after Amy was born, even that had been too demanding a role, and Serena had left work to become a full-time mom.

But her time there had been a rewarding one, as she'd become good friends with the bishop. Knowing her strengths as he did, he had gotten into the habit of suggesting her as a fill preacher when clergy around the diocese took their much-needed vacations. Later, when the girls were firmly established in school, he began using Gemma as an interim at parishes around the Seattle area.

Now, standing in the doorway of the bishop's familiar mahogany-paneled office, she watched as he stood slowly and came around his desk. He was starting to show his age, she thought with surprise. He'd always had a young heart, but now she could see he was definitely looking stooped. He settled himself into the leather chair beside the defunct fireplace with its Rookwood tile and gestured her into the armchair opposite.

"Have you ever been to Brandon's Rock?" he asked.

"You know, I always wanted to go there," she confided. "It intrigued me, the way so many members of the congregation would show up for Cathedral Day. They seemed to have an awful lot of energy for such a small parish in such a remote location."

Brandon's Rock was a small island off the coast of western Washington State, part of the state's beautiful San Juan Islands. Originally a summer retreat for wealthy Seattleites, the island boasted only a few hundred year-round residents, a mix of retired doctors and lawyers and the construction folk and local workers who mended their roads, manned the restaurants and coffee shops, built and repaired summer homes, and provided rudimentary services during the summer months, when the population swelled to double its normal size.

The little stone church on the island, St. Aidan's-by-the-Sea, had been built by the notorious lumber baron Elwood Bartenstein in the early 1920's, to commemorate a son lost in the mission field. Over the years the original family had continued to maintain the church, and various other islanders had contributed to its upkeep, but when the God-is-dead movement hit in the sixties the baron's heirs had found better things to do with their money, and the church had fallen on hard times.

"You know I believe," said the bishop, "that a church's character is set early. The people at St. Aidan's – or perhaps we should call it St. Elwood's, as the rest of the island does -- are good folk, really they are. But their last priest was a mistake, and they -- and the church, and, I suspect, the community – have paid dearly for that.

"They're holding on," he continued, "but just barely. The physical plant seems to face a new crisis every month, and the congregation is aging and dwindling rapidly. I think there's a lot of potential there, but there will probably need to be some fairly serious changes if the church is to survive. And I suspect – though I will leave it to you to decide – that the first thing to change will need to be the ousting of the senior warden."

"Her name is Marcia Breezley," the bishop went on, "and she's been warden now through three priests – the good, the bad, and the ugly. She has a good heart," he said, "but she rules that parish with an iron fist. Unfortunately she's squeezing the life out of it." *Clearly*, Gemma thought as she stared unseeing out the window, listening to Marcia drone on about parish lists and budget concerns, *the bishop was right. She's already squeezing the life out of me, and I only just got here!*

CHAPTER 2

Looking away from the window, Gemma reached in her briefcase for her favorite pad of paper and a felt-tipped pen. Obviously, from Marcia Breezley's point of view, St. Elwood's was going to Hell in a handbasket, and Gemma was just the weight to sink it the rest of the way down.

"I'll be honest with you," Marcia said, pacing back and forth on the worn carpet in Gemma's office, "I don't know what the bishop was thinking, sending a woman here. He *knows* this church is more conservative than that. At least a man could help fix our plumbing problems."

"Well, I don't know what to tell you about that, though I'm happy to discuss the theology behind women's ordination if you want to hear about it. And you're right; I've no aptitude for plumbing. But I'm pretty good with computers and xerox machines, if you have any of those," Gemma said, looking around hopefully.

Marcia humphed at that and walked over to peer out the window. "There's that Morgan boy wandering loose again. I don't know what his mother is thinking; he should be in school." She opened the window and yelled out at a boy who sat on the beach below, idly skipping rocks. "You there! Jasper! Get off that beach; don't you know this is private property?" The boy looked up at the window, shrugged, and continued skipping stones. Gemma made a mental note to look into Jasper's situation once her meeting with Marcia was done.

"Now, first off," said Marcia, "we need to focus on the service on Sunday. It's a bit of a novelty having a woman preacher here. Some of the parishioners probably won't come; they're the ones that wrote the bishop to complain when he told us you would be assigned as our interim.

"But there's probably just as many people that have never seen a woman priest before; most folks assume Episcopal priests are all male and celibate, like the Catholic ones. So we're bound to get a few curiosity seekers. You'll need to have greeters at the door who can tell the regular members from those folks; we'll need to put the visitors near the back so it'll be easy for them to leave once they realize it's just an ordinary service."

"So what constitutes an ordinary service here?" asked Gemma.

"Well, Agnes -- she's our organist, you know -- she plays a little prelude while the pews are filling up, and then we always march in to Hymn No. 108 – 'Rock of Ages.' Then you'll stand up and give the announcements; I'll hand you the list before you walk in. Harry Borden does the Old Testament reading and leads the Psalm.

"We get another hymn (you can choose that one, there are several that we rotate through), you read the Gospel, give us a short sermon – five minutes should do it -- then Harry leads the prayers of the people, you do the communion, and with a couple of verses of 'Onward Christian Soldiers' we're out of here. Agnes has some real nice flourishes for that one."

"And do you work off the Lectionary passages?" asked Gemma.

"What's a lectionary?"

"Never mind," said Gemma. "So how does Harry choose what Bible passages to read?"

"I think he just picks whatever seems appropriate... I make suggestions, of course," replied Marcia, thrusting her chin forward.

"I see," said Gemma. "Is that how the services are always done here?"

"Oh, yes," said Marcia. "Except Christmas and Easter, of course. At Christmas we get Christmas carols instead of hymns, and for Easter we always do 'I Come to the Garden Alone,' "The Old Rugged Cross' and 'Were You There When They Crucified My Lord.' "

"Hmmm," said Gemma. "And where can I find Agnes?"

"Oh, you can usually find her out at the house; she gives piano lessons most afternoons after school."

"I see," said Gemma. "Who takes care of the altar – flowers, bread, wine, that sort of thing?"

"That would be me," said Marcia, preening slightly. "Unless I'm sick, then Mae Dorrington does the flowers, but of course her garden never quite measures up to mine. Father Parkinson ordered the wine by the case; we have that all stored down on the basement so you just have to bring up a bottle Sunday morning. And we get those little dried wafer things; Joyce has an automatic order in for those."

"I see," said Gemma. "Does no one ever bake bread for communion?"

"I should say not!" said Marcia. "If wafers were good enough for the Lord, they're good enough for St. Elwood's!"

"Ah," said Gemma. "Well, that should be enough to get us through this Sunday. I gather there aren't enough children to hold a Sunday school; is there anything else I need to deal with right now? I know you have a whole list of larger concerns – the roof, the kitchen – and the plumbing, apparently. How about if we schedule another meeting later this week and you can put together a complete list for me; we'll see if we can get that prioritized before the vestry meeting next Tuesday."

Mrs. Breezley looked a little huffy at being hustled out of Gemma's office so summarily, but was apparently appeased by the thought of the list and the next meeting. "Shall we say Thursday at 2? She asked. "Orville always goes down for his nap then."

"Thursday at 2 will be fine, Mrs. Breezley," said Gemma, and she shut the door firmly behind her. She waited until she heard the outer door slam, and then dialed the bishop's private number.

"Bishop Farwell," he answered.

"You owe me one, Sam. How could you do this to me? She's impossible!"

"Gemma, is that you?"

"Of course it's me, you old buzzard. What were you thinking putting me in here? They haven't changed a thing since 1950; it's a wonder this place is still standing. And I hate to think what's going to happen when I try to flush the toilet."

"Hang in there, Gemma. God called you to this parish, not me. I'm sure She knew exactly what She was doing."

"Don't get funny with me, Sam. Do you have any idea what they *do* here? When's the last time you did a visitation in this godforsaken parish?"

"Now, now, Gemma; no parish is godforsaken. God watches over *all* her parishes, I'm sure, even the ones that have no clue She's a female."

"You're avoiding the subject, Sam. When was your last visitation to Brandon's Rock? Oh, no. Let me guess. You've never even been to Brandon's Rock, have you? You let old Bishop Harrison take care of them, didn't you. Chicken. And now you send me in to do your dirty work. What the *Hell* were you thinking?"

"Come on, Gemma. A call is a call. There's a reason you're there; the timing was too perfect. I'm counting on you – *God* is counting on you – to bring those lovely people into the 21st century. Now stop whining and start preaching; if anyone can do this, you can. Gotta run, see ya, keep in touch!"… and the bishop hung up on her.

Gemma returned the receiver to its cradle and dropped her head into her hands. *Oh, God,* she prayed. *Where do I begin?*

CHAPTER 3

That Wednesday night the winds came down out of the north, bringing biting cold and heavy rains, leaving no doubt in Gemma's mind of the church's need for a new roof. Not only were there several puddles on the (thankfully) stone sanctuary floor, but the list she had been compiling and had left on her desk was muddied beyond recognition; her favorite lilac legal tablet destroyed. The only good thing was that the water had all been absorbed by the tablet so the desk, though it had obviously seen better days, was relatively unharmed.

With the help of two women in matching pink sweatsuits whom she found splitting tulip and daffodil bulbs in the church garden, Gemma was able to move the desk to an apparently leak-free corner. They also reassured her that the first rain was always the worst.

"The cedar shakes on the roof dry out over the summer," said the sturdy blonde one, whose name was Carol. "Once the rains come they swell up and then the roof is much tighter." The other woman, who needed some help standing after kneeling in the garden, turned out to be Carol's mother, Eileen.

"Oh, yes," Eileen warbled, "Elwood used that excuse for years to put off getting a new roof on our house."

"Elwood?" queried Gemma. "That wouldn't be the Elwood of St. Elwood's, would it?"

"Oh, no," trilled Eileen, "that was my Elwood's great-grandfather. My Elwood, he's Elwood the 4th, he came along long after that family tree dried up. He was illegitimate, you know, kinda like Carol here. His mama was the town tramp and his daddy got disinherited after he refused to marry her. Oh, he was a wild one, my Elwood," she smiled, reminiscing. "Started a commune here in the '70's – that's where I met him. Smoked up 'til the day he died, Elwood did."

"Oh," said Gemma. "Did he die of cancer?"

"Oh, no, honey, he wasn't a cigarette smoker; it was pot! And he didn't die of cancer; he got hit by a drunk driving a pickup one Saturday night when he was motorcycling home from the Men's Retreat."

"Mom!" chimed Carol.

"Oh, honey, don't fret yourself," said Eileen. "Pastor Gemma looks like she's probly heard worse. You have a husband honey?" she asked.

"Yes, Alex. He's a pediatrician; he decided to spend this year in India working for Doctors without Borders, now that our two daughters are off at college."

"Needed a little break, did you? Parenting teenagers can be hard on a relationship...?"

"Oh no, it's not like that," Gemma smiled. "It's just that we were in the Peace Corps together after we were married, and Alex has always wanted to go back. But I feel I can make more of a difference in the world by helping our churches grow and thrive. A lot of good work overseas is funded by churches no bigger than St. Elwood's; they're just packed with people passionate to make a difference."

"Wow," said Eileen, looking at Gemma with new eyes. "You're not at all like that Father Parkinson. I'd almost be willing to go to church if someone like you was preaching."

"Oh," said Gemma, "you mean you're not members?"

"Oh, no, not us," said Carol. "We're not really the religious type, ya know what I mean?"

"Um, I guess so," said Gemma. "But then why are you here?"

"Oh," said Eileen, "we're in the Brandon's Rock Garden Club. Part of the BBR – that's Beautify Brandon's Rock – Charter is we rotate care of all the public gardens; it was just our turn to do the church."

"Ah," said Gemma. "I see. Well, then, don't let me keep you."

"No problem," Eileen reassured her. "We was about done anyway; my knees were startin' to go. Good luck with everything; maybe we'll see you at the market sometime."

"Yeah," said Carol. "And good luck with that Marcia Breezley!" Both women giggled as they gathered up the remaining bulbs and their tools into a box and stuffed it all in the back of a rusty purple pickup. "Bye, now," they waved, and they climbed in and drove away.

When Gemma walked back into the church there was a thin woman with extremely black hair standing in front of the filing cabinet outside her office. "Hi, you must be Joyce," said Gemma, holding out her hand. Marcia and the bishop had both mentioned that Joyce Finley was the church secretary, but Gemma hadn't seen anyone touch Joyce's desk or files since she'd arrived on Monday. "I'm Gemma Benson, your new interim vicar."

"Nice to meet you," said Joyce shyly. "I'm sorry I haven't been around lately; my daughter's been sick. Did we get too much damage from that rain last night? I've already mopped up the puddles in the sanctuary."

"Thanks," said Gemma. "I'd have done that but I've been busy repairing the damage in my office."

"Oh, dear, I should have thought of that: we moved your desk for the exterminator and we forgot to put it back. I hope things weren't too bad."

"Exterminator?" enquired Gemma.

"Nothing serious," said Joyce. "Just a little rat problem; they were going after the communion wafers, which we'd been leaving in your office since Father Parkinson left."

"I see," said Gemma. "And where are you storing them now?"

"Oh, we put them in the safe; for sure the rats can't get in there! So, have you made a decision yet about which hymn to use on Sunday?"

"What are my choices?"

"Well, I figure since this Sunday is Veteran's Day you'll probably want 'The Battle Hymn of the Republic.'"

"Really," said Gemma.

"Oh, yes, Father Parkinson always used that one for the military holidays – you know, Veterans Day, Memorial Day, Presidents Day, stuff like that."

"I see. Well, we'll let that stand for now, I guess. I should probably go work on the sermon for Sunday – unless that's already in place as well?"

"Oh, no; we let the vicar take care of that. Just be sure you don't go over five minutes, though; Orville Breezley has low blood pressure, and if you go more than 5 minutes he falls asleep and he's a bear to wake up."

"I see; I'll try to make allowances for that then," said Gemma, and she went into her office and shut the door.

CHAPTER 4

Thursday evening found Gemma at home in the little cabin the church had arranged for her to rent for the year. Exhausted from her afternoon's meeting with Mrs. Breezley, she'd heated a frozen pepperoni pizza for dinner, and was now seated at her laptop, trying to hammer out some sort of sermon.

Venice, who had enjoyed a busy day chasing songbirds and small rodents, dozed contentedly, twitching occasionally as he dreamed on the fleece bed Gemma had placed on the desk behind her computer. A fire crackled merrily in the woodstove in the next room, and one of her favorite CDs from Anonymous 4 murmured softly in the background. Scratching absently at the leg of her sweatpants, Gemma was trying to find a shorter way to relate the widow's mite to Veterans Day and the challenges facing St. Elwood's when the phone rang.

"Mother Benson," trilled Marcia Breezley's imperious voice over the line.

"Yes," said Gemma warily.

"I'm afraid you'll need to come down to the church right away," said Mrs. Breezley. "Stop that this instant!" Gemma heard her say to someone nearby, and the phone dropped with a loud clatter. Grabbing her coat and keys, Gemma ran out the door and drove as fast as she dared down the long winding road into town, praying Mrs. Breezley was all right.

She arrived to find all the lights on in the sanctuary, and Mrs. Breezley holding the little boy from the beach, Jasper, by the hood of his coat. Jasper took advantage of Mrs. Breezley's distraction at her arrival to twist out of his coat, and ran for the door. Gemma caught the boy in her arms and, holding him firmly, squatted down to his level to get eye contact. "What's up, big guy," she asked, and to her surprise the boy, instead of twisting to get away again, dissolved into tears.

"What seems to be the problem, Marcia?" Gemma asked.

"I was driving by the church after Bridge Night," said Marcia. "We meet every other Thursday at the Senior Center, you know. And I saw a light moving in the sanctuary. So I said to myself, Marcia, somebody's up to no good and it's up to you to stop it. So I cut my lights, pulled into the handicap spot and came into the sanctuary to find this young man stacking up the pew cushions."

"I didn't mean to, Miss," wailed the boy. "It's just that it was so cold, and I thought if I had enough cushions it might keep me warmer."

"But why were you in the sanctuary in the first place?" asked Gemma.

Jasper dropped his head and bit his lip, refusing to speak.

"What's the matter with you, boy?" asked Marcia. "Cat got your tongue? Or has that no-good mother of yours run off again?"

"She's not no good," wailed Jasper. "I just can't find the key."

"What key, dear?" asked Gemma, wiping a tear from the boy's cheek. *He could have been mine*, she thought, and a familiar ache welled up in her heart for the little boy she had lost in childbirth back all those years ago.

"Tell me, please." Gemma said again, "what key?"

"It's the key to our trailer, mum. She usually keeps it under the flowerpot by the door, but it's not there and the door's locked and I didn't know where else to go."

"How did you get in here?" Marcia asked in forbidding tones.

"Th-There's a secret way in through the basement," said Jasper. "The big boys send me in there sometimes to raid Father Parkinson's wine, 'cuz I'm the only one that can fit."

"Hmm," said Gemma, looking up at Mrs. Breezley. "Looks like we have a couple more things to add to that list of yours."

She stood, keeping a careful grip on Jasper's shoulder. "I think you can go home now, Mrs. Breezley. I'll see this young man has a warm bed for the night, and we'll talk again on Sunday. I'm sure your husband is wondering what's become of you."

"Oh, that Orville, he'll have been in bed long since," said Marcia. "He always goes to bed early on bridge nights. Now don't you let that boy take advantage of you now; best to call child protective services and let them deal with him."

Jasper struggled mightily at that, but Gemma wrapped her other arm around him and said to the departing Marcia, "Plenty of time for that. Right now let's get him warmed and fed. Let me guess," she said, squatting down again after Marcia left, slamming the door behind her, "Did you get supper tonight, Jasper?"

"No, miss," the boy replied. "Nor lunch, neither. Mom made me a sandwich before she left, but old man Lindquist's dog got it when I was walking to school. Took it right out of my hand, he did; like to scared me half to death."

"Who is old man Lindquist?" Gemma asked, as she doused the lights and locked the church door, then walked to her car to tuck Jasper into the passenger seat.

"Well, they say he's a scientist, mum, but I don't know about that. He looks a little crazy, with his troll hair all sticking up. And that dog of his is a right mean 'un, he is."

"What sort of dog is it?" Gemma asked, as she put her Subaru into gear, backed out of the church parking lot and headed back up the island.

"I don't rightly know, mum. But he's big, and one of his ears sticks up and the other lies down, and he's real fast."

"Well, perhaps I'll speak with Mr. Lindquist tomorrow about his dog," said Gemma. "But right now let's get you home and fed. I have some leftover pizza; how does that sound?"

"Great!" said Jasper.

"And you're sure your mother won't be worrying about you?" Gemma asked.

"Oh, no, mum. Thursday's her night to stay late on the Mainland," Jasper replied. "Thursdays and Saturdays I'm always on my own."

"I see," said Gemma. "And what about your dad?"

"Oh, he lives in Montana," replied the boy. "I'm sposed to visit every summer, but this year I ran away so I missed the plane. Mom weren't much pleased about that, but I hate Montana," he muttered. "Not going there again. I won't, and she can't make me." The boy crossed his arms and stared resolutely out the window of Gemma's car, watching the trees go by in the darkness. She saw a hand come up and surreptitiously wipe a cheek, but said nothing.

"I hope you're not allergic to cats," she said as they pulled into the driveway of her cabin. "Because my Venice likes nothing better than to snuggle with strangers."

"Oh, no, mum. Cats and me, we get along real well, 'cept sometimes they scratch."

"Well, yes, that's probably because you pet them too much," said Gemma as they walked up to her front door. "Venice will do that, too, if you're not careful." She opened the door and beckoned Jasper into the inviting warmth. "There he is now. Ah, Venice, look, someone new for you to lick!"

Venice immediately stretched his paws up Jasper's pantleg, and the delighted boy sank to the floor.

"I'll just heat up that pizza for you," said Gemma, heading into the kitchen.

"Oh, no, mum," said Jasper, "I like it fine cold. That's mostly how I get it anyway," he added.

"I see," said Gemma. And she was afraid she did.

CHAPTER 5

On Friday morning, Gemma made French toast for herself and Jasper, who had never had real Canadian maple syrup before. She dropped him off at school on her way to the church, then rolled into the parking lot to find all the spaces filled, even the ones for the handicapped.

Parking across the street in the drugstore lot, Gemma walked over to the church and peered in. The pews were full, and a woman was standing at the front of the church describing what sounded like an extremely interesting weekend. Gemma went down the side aisle and out to the church office, where Joyce sat, diligently typing what appeared to be Sunday's bulletin.

"I see we have an AA chapter meeting here," guessed Gemma.

"Oh, yes, Mother Benson. They meet every Friday morning on one of the islands; first Friday is always here on Brandon's Rock. I'm not sure what they'll do now that Father Parkinson isn't here to lead them."

"Please," said Gemma, "call me Gemma. Was Father Parkinson a member?"

"Oh, yes, Mother—I mean, Gemma. 'Course he was always falling off the wagon, though you could kinda tell when one of his bad spells was coming. He and Mavis Grantham – Mrs. Borden, that was, before Harry divorced her for partying too much with Father Parkinson – they'd get to giggling down in the basement with all the communion wine and I'd know to call old Father Jordan on Lopez Island to take over the Sunday service."

"Interesting," said Gemma. "And how long had this been going on before Father Parkinson left?"

"Oh, off and on 'bout four years. Nobody minded too much except Harry, but he got spittin' mad when Mavis and Father crashed up his RV. He set a lot of store by that RV, took it fishing with Tom, the postmaster, every fall. They never were able to get it up outta that gully, although, course, Mavis and Father were so drunk they just rolled right out of it and staggered on home."

"I see," said Gemma. "And that was when Harry called the bishop?"

"Oh, no; he didn't call the bishop 'til Mavis and Father accidentally set fire to the lodge."

"The lodge?" asked Gemma.

"Well, it was really just a guest cottage. But Harry built it himself outta logs from his own property, and decorated it with all them deer heads he killed at the annual deer shoot? So he was pretty pissed when Mavis and Father burned it down– if you'll pardon my language."

"No problem," said Gemma. "So wrecking the RV was okay, but setting fire to the lodge was the last straw?"

"Yes'm," said Joyce. "That's when he called the bishop. And let me tell you, there was a hootin' and a hollerin' at that vestry meeting when they announced Father was leaving."

"Really," said Gemma. "Father Parkinson was upset?"

"Oh, no, mum. It was the vestry that was upset. Father Parkinson had been hosting the monthly vestry pool parties down in the Sunday school room, and when he left he took the pool table with him."

"Ah," said Gemma. "I see. Well, then. Don't let me keep you."

"Oh, no problem, Mother – I mean, Gemma. There's not much to doing the bulletin; only the one hymn and the date to change. We never actually put in the Bible readings, because Harry just kinda threw out whatever seemed appropriate to the occasion. The Sunday after the fire at the lodge the reading was that Revelation passage, you know, the one about committing fornication, the smoke of her burning, judgment has come…"

"Hmm," said Gemma. "Just out of curiosity, what did he read the Sunday after Father and Mavis tipped the RV into the gully?"

"Oh, I believe that one was Jeremiah," said Joyce, "the one that goes "were they ashamed? No, therefore they shall fall among the fallen."

"I see. Well then, carry on Joyce."

"Yes'm," said Joyce, and soon Gemma could hear the rhythmic churning of the office Xerox machine.

Sitting at her desk, Gemma stared at the sermon she had finished editing the night before and sighed. No longer a white-knuckled seminarian, determined to preach all she knew in her first sermon, she nonetheless sensed that the circumstances she was gradually uncovering at St. Elwood's called for something different, something a bit... unorthodox. Time for a little Eugene Peterson, she thought, setting aside her previous night's efforts, and she reached into her briefcase and pulled out *The Message*, Peterson's radical interpretation of the Scriptures.

Perhaps hearing the Bible in their own language would jolt the parishioners of St. Elwood's out of their comfortable pews, she thought. Something sure needed to do it. She shook her head and, chewing on her pencil, began thumbing through the pages of *The Message*, looking for the Mark passage she'd be sharing with St. Elwood's this coming Sunday.

CHAPTER 6

When Gemma crawled into bed late Saturday night she was exhausted, and not much closer to her five-minute sermon than she'd been the previous afternoon. A storm had blown up out of the south Friday evening, and it had rained all day Saturday. The church and her office had, true to predictions, stayed dry, but for some reason the basement floor of the little cabin she had rented for the year was two inches deep in water.

Gemma suspected, given the whitish stains on the earthenware tiles in the downstairs guest room, that this was not the first time the floor down there had been covered with water. But her landlord claimed it had never happened before, and implied that it was somehow her fault and her responsibility to solve the issue.

At Joyce's suggestion she had called the Urbizo Brothers, and Carlo Urbizo had arrived, shaking his head and scratching his rather protuberant belly as he checked out the rising water problem.

"Can't install a sump pump 'til the water goes down," he'd said, "but I think I can rig up something for you. Got a spare bilge pump in the truck." Gemma served as plumber's assistant while Carlo set up a car battery on the workbench in the storeroom across from the flooded guestroom and ran a wire from the battery to the bilge pump, which would continue working as long as it was submerged. Together they set up a complicated series of PVC pipes that stretched from the bilge pump across the basement floor and out the back door.

"Won't work too well if the wind picks up," said Carlo. "But we don't usually get the heavy winds 'til December, and by then we should be able to get the sump pump installed for ya."

Of course, as soon as Carlo left the wind had kicked up; Gemma had to round up some rope off the beach to tie down the back door to keep it from banging back and forth and dislodging the tenuously connected pipes. With the door propped open to accommodate the pipes, the basement had gotten incredibly cold; at this rate she'd be able to invite Jasper over to skate on the guest room floor.

The rest of the house was growing increasingly chilled as well. She'd closed the door at the bottom of the stairs, but the moist cold seemed to seep up through the flooring, and she was grateful for the heated mattress pad and flannel sheets that Alex had recommended she bring with her to Brandon's Rock.

Oh, Alex, Gemma thought, missing him as she burrowed under the covers, fortified with a late night sherry, two pairs of socks and fleece pajamas. *I wish you were here.*

They had exchanged emails earlier in the day, and after reading his description of his boat ride to the little island off the southern tip of India with the charming Italian family, she was beginning to wonder if perhaps the heat, dust and dung of India might not be preferable, after all, to the icy cold and pastoral shenanigans of Brandon's Rock.

Alex, of course, had been greatly amused by the soap-operatic tales of Father Parkinson's adventures. "Just remember, dear," he'd noted at the end of his last email, "You can't fix everything at once. Try to keep the big picture in mind and just move them along in baby steps. That's the way it is here at the hospital, too. The sanitary conditions here are simply untenable, but we just have to fix things one step at a time."

Amy and Serena had written as well, full of stories of their Halloween adventures at college (for Amy) and in Taiwan (for Serena). Gemma had shipped them each a care package full of Halloween goodies, and she was pleased to learn that both packages had arrived in plenty of time for the festivities. "But Mom," Serena had added, "I don't think they even know what Halloween *is* here! My classmates loved all the candy, though – which is a good thing, because Darwin and Mick (her boyfriend and their roommate) refused to eat all that junkfood..."

As Gemma drifted off to sleep, lulled by the hum of the bilge pump working away in the room below her bed, she found herself hoping God wouldn't desert her here on Brandon's Rock. She'd fallen asleep many times before on a Saturday night after a week of study with no sermon to show for it, and so far she'd always awakened with an image on Sunday morning that would crystallize the sermon for her.

There was no reason to assume God wouldn't bless her that way again, but Gemma had been preaching – and living – long enough to understand that, as her father used to say, "The Lord pays in strange money." There was no question in Gemma's mind that the Lord would answer her prayers. The question was only whether she would appreciate – or even understand – the answer she got.

But, true to form, Gemma awakened early Sunday morning; it was only a little after 5 when she crawled out of bed. The wind had died down and the house seemed a little warmer. Venice hovered underfoot, complaining constantly until she put food in his bowl, then munched contentedly in the corner while she poured leftover coffee into her favorite cup – a relic from an old Anglican ad campaign, with an image of the earth from space and the slogan, "Not Working Right? Speak with the Original Owner."

She popped the cup into the microwave, punched in one minute, and pushed start, but nothing happened. She checked the plug and the outlet, then went down to the now-dry basement to investigate the breaker switches, but all seemed to be in order. Since the floor down there was dry, she disconnected the pump and the pipes and closed the door, then went back upstairs to make a fresh pot of coffee, making made a mental note to email her landlord about the microwave.

Ah, she thought, amazed and delighted as always by the mysterious workings of the Lord and the human mind. *There it is! That's my sermon!*

The coffee was a minor inconvenience, affecting no one but herself, yet it was enough to throw her whole morning off. So how amazing was it, she thought, for our veterans and their families, to risk their entire lives in the service of their countries? Their sacrifice is incredible: instead of spending our energies worrying about our own minor problems, we should be inspired by the sacrifice of our veterans, and be willing to follow their example and take risks for the benefit of the whole community.

St. Elwood's parishioners were too caught up in their own problems – the faulty kitchen, the leaky roof, the plumbing – and too attached to their own way of doing things. They really should take inspiration from our veterans, she thought, and instead of focusing on their own physical plant, think about something they could do that might benefit, not just the parish, but the whole community.

The godly life, the exemplary life, she thought, is not about playing it safe. It's about making the world a better place, about giving back, about working for the larger good. After all, as Einstein said, only a life lived for others is a life worthwhile.

The folks at St. Elwood's had been doing "microwave church" for years now, nuking the same old tired hymns and stories and outdated liturgies. Perhaps it might be time to brew up a fresh pot. Same basic flavor, but maybe with time she could introduce some exciting new options.

Caramel Macchiato, she thought, warming to her subject. *I never understood what a caramel macchiato is, but it sounds absolutely delicious. Mocha, vanilla, grande, venti, breve – the possibilities were endless. Surely, together, they could find a flavor of church that would not only perk up the current congregation, but bring in some new customers with a taste for adventure.*

God, thought Gemma. *What I wouldn't give for one of those pumpkin-flavored latte's right now. But I'm getting ahead of myself. Let's just make the initial suggestion for now. After all, I'm only an interim; it's their congregation, and it's up to them to figure out what flavor they want to be.*

Conservative, liberal, Rite I, Rite II, Message, King James, sherry, wine, bread, wafers, guitars, organ… Today's Episcopal Church had a lot of latitude. The parishioners of St. Elwood's needed a chance to explore their options away from the tight-fisted leadership of Marcia Breezley. But first Gemma would need to whet their appetite without completely alienating them.

What to do, what to do. Gemma sat at her little kitchen table with its traditional red and white checked oilcloth cover, nursing her coffee and drumming her fingers. What would be something really small, some tiny shift from the norm, that they might actually enjoy, these people who had stood by and watched their priest drinking and cavorting with a parishioner and never complained.

I know, thought Gemma. *They always come to Cathedral Day. What if I started now convincing them to plan for that? Maybe if I suggested to the bishop that this year's theme should be the varieties of Anglican Worship, and then convinced them to take field trips to spy on other congregations?*

Gemma's brain continued to churn. Getting them off-island might be tricky. Was there some anniversary they could celebrate, some special service they could plan, and maybe study up for? They needed to be able to take pride in St. Elwood's.

Maybe all I need to do is ... I know. Get them to prepare a video of a worship service to show potential clergy! But before they can do that, maybe I can get them samples of other parish videos. That way they can see for themselves that there's more than one way to get a delicious cup of coffee.

And with that, Gemma poured herself another cup, turned off the pot, and began her preparations for the Sunday service.

CHAPTER 7

Of course, thought Gemma, standing, robed in white for the service, in the vestibule outside St. Elwood's imposing stone and timber sanctuary. Straightening her stole as Agnes the organist pounded through the introductory strains of Rock of Ages, she cast a sideways glance at Harry Borden, who was making some last-minute adjustments to his cincture. *I bet they sing 'Rock of Ages' at every service because they think it's about Brandon's Rock. So that's one part of the service they'll for sure be stubborn about changing.* Gemma watched as Joyce's daughter Darla took up the ceremonial cross and led the way down the aisle to the altar.

Walking down the aisle and singing, Gemma noted that the pews were about as full as they were anywhere else in the Diocese for an 8 am Rite I service – except, of course, that this was actually a 10 am Rite I service. *What ever made the bishop think these people would tolerate a woman priest?* she wondered. *They still think they're "not worthy so much as to gather up the crumbs under God's table."*

Fortunately Gemma had grown up attending a Rite I service with her grandmother, so the familiar melodious words came easily to her. "Blessed be God, Father, Son and Holy Spirit," she intoned when she reached the altar (at least it wasn't back against the wall, she thought. Apparently some enterprising and forward-looking priest had seen fit to bring the altar forward. Perhaps by suggesting it was "Popish" to leave it back against the wall?) "And blessed be his kingdom, now and forever," the congregation duly responded, and the Sunday service began.

Harry wasn't a bad reader, she thought, as she watched him recite the Old Testament lesson and lead the congregation through the Psalms. He was a tall and extremely thin man, with a long face, a very prominent Adam's Apple, and a distracting habit of cracking his neck at the end of every verse. But his voice was deep and surprisingly sonorous, and Gemma reveled in it for a moment, closing her eyes and listening as the familiar words of the 23rd Psalm filled the sanctuary and settled in the inverted boat-shaped timbers that formed St. Elwood's high cathedral ceiling.

"And I will dwell in the House of the Lord forever" Harry intoned with a final crick of his neck, and he sat down. *Well,* thought Gemma, as the last words of the Psalm soared up, *Grandmother always said "Begin as you mean to continue."* So she rose, walked down the altar steps to stand in the aisle about three rows back, holding the huge leather Bible aloft before her. "The Holy Gospel of our Lord Jesus Christ, according to Mark," she said, and she heard the faint rustle of genuflection as the congregation recited back, "Glory be to thee, O Lord."

The day's gospel lesson, Mark 12: 38-44, was the story of the widow's mite, but it began with some rather unfortunate observations from Jesus about "scribes who like to go about in long robes…and to have the best seats in the churches and the places of honor at feasts." She sincerely hoped no one thought she was deliberately attacking Marcia, sitting there with Orville in the front row.

When she finished reading the Gospel passage, Gemma returned to the lectern and placed the Bible on its stand. "Let us pray," she said, and the members of the congregation who had begun to settle into their pews rose hurriedly again and bowed their heads, eyeing Gemma somewhat anxiously. Would she be one of those priests who prayed long beseeching prayers? But then, perhaps not, given that the Gospel lesson had just condemned those who "for a pretense make long prayers."

"Bless the words of my mouth, and us to thy service, O Lord. Amen," said Gemma, and with a sigh of relief the parishioners echoed her Amen and sat.

Gemma kept her sermon brief, focusing on the importance of the widow's mite and the relative value of sacrificial giving; of giving "extravagantly" from the heart rather than for the sake of appearances. She cited the generosity of our veterans – who had been willing to give their all, even their lives -- as an example and warned against getting caught up in appearances.

"So you see," said Gemma at the end of her remarks, "what St. Elwood's needs more than a bigger budget, or a new roof, or a new kitchen, or more efficient plumbing, is to find a sense of mission, a way to give of itself to this community and beyond. Former Archbishop of Canterbury William Temple once said that the Church is the only institution on earth which exists for the sake of those who are not its members. I believe that if we here at St. Elwood's concentrate on giving rather than on receiving, the other challenges we face will be resolved. If we operate out of a sense of abundance, like the widow in the story, abundance and blessing will be ours.

"And now," she said, taking a deep breath, "I wanted to speak with you about something else. As your interim vicar, I'm only going to be here a year. And somehow over the course of that year we're going to need to put together a packet of materials that will explain how unique St. Elwood's is, so that you can find a wonderful priest who will appreciate all of you and take over here when I leave.

"I'm thinking one of the best ways to do that would be to have someone here videotape a sampling of what gives you pride in St. Elwood's. We could show pictures of the church and its people, samples of your worship together, and include some footage of parishioners involved in Cathedral Day, and maybe we can add some sort of community ministry, so your new priest can see that you are more than just a beautiful building.

"Now I'm sure you'll want to put your best foot forward," added Gemma. "So I've asked the folks at the diocesan resource center to put together a sampling of similar videos from other congregations around the diocese, so you can get an idea of how this might look. Plus I've invited some other churches around the diocese to share some of their practices with us. Who knows? You might find there's something they do that interests you; some combination of music and liturgy, some kind of worship or community service that you think might really become a passion for our parishioners. It's my hope that in watching these videos and imagining a new future for St. Elwood's we will be able to work together to find new ways to serve the community of Brandon's Rock.

"…and I've said these things to you in the name of the father, and of the Son, and of the Holy Spirit," Gemma concluded, and she turned and strode back to the altar. "Please stand and join me in saying together the Nicene Creed," she said, and the communion portion of the service began.

The remainder of the morning went off without a hitch, although there was a little awkwardness during the Passing of the Peace. Apparently Father Parkinson had been in the habit of coming out into the congregation and hugging all the women, and when Gemma remained up on the dais several of the men looked like they might be ready to come up after her, so she came down and duly hugged her new parishioners.

After the last chords of 'Onward Christian Soldiers' had faded away, Gemma stood in the vestibule and greeted her departing flock. Most had kind words to say about the service, and several were eager to offer suggestions for the video and the ministry. Gemma carefully noted their names and suggestions, filing them away for later when she would put together a planning committee for the project. And afterwards, as they were disrobing in the sacristy, Harry shyly mentioned that he had some skill with the video camera and might be able to help with the tape production.

"Excellent," said Gemma, seeing the perfect opening. "Why don't I put you on the video committee – and Mrs. Breezley, of course, and perhaps a few of the vestry members? We can plan to spend an evening sometime soon watching those videos I ordered from the diocesan resource center."

"That would be fine," said Harry, hanging up his alb. Gemma hung hers beside it, marveling a little at the difference in length between the two robes.

"Great, Harry," she said. "And thanks for your help with the service today. I can see you've been doing a lot to hold this place together."

"Thanks," said Harry, shrugging into his coat.

"Harry," said Gemma on impulse as he headed out the door. "Could I interest you in a cup of coffee?"

"Why, yes," said Harry, cricking his neck nervously.

"Is there a place you prefer to go?" asked Gemma

"Oh, Jonie's would be fine," said Harry.

"Great," said Gemma. "Let me get my things out of the office. I'll just be a minute, and we can walk up together."

Though the sun appeared to have taken its usual November vacation, the harsh winds of Friday had died down, the air was warmer, and there was a pleasant scrunching of leaves underfoot as they walked up the block or so to Jonie's diner.

Gemma hadn't been to Jonie's before, though she knew it was an institution on Brandon's Rock. She was disappointed to find they didn't serve latte or espressos, but as she slid down the picnic bench that served as a seat she reflected that the coffee wasn't bad, for regular coffee. She took another sip and looked up at Harry, seated across from her, looking somewhat morose. Not surprising, she thought, given that, thanks to Father Parkinson, he was now living alone.

"So, Harry," she said. "I know we have a vestry meeting coming up on Tuesday, And I've certainly gotten an earful from Marcia about what needs to be done around here. But I'm sure you have a different perspective on things. I mean, you've been doing the readings and assisting with communion for … how many years is it now?"

"Well," said Harry, "I guess it depends on how you count. I began assisting as an acolyte when I was nine…"

"In this church?" queried Gemma.

"Oh, yes. My grandparents settled here back when the Indians were still using the island for their pow-wows. My dad remembers hiding under the bed when they came to visit the house for the shellfish negotiations."

"My goodness," said Gemma. "I had no idea! I know you used to be married; had your wife grown up here as well?"

"Oh, no," said Harry. "I met her when I went off-island to the U. She was real pretty then; I didn't think I was good enough for her. But she followed me back here and we've lived on the island ever since; got married at St. Elwood's in the spring of '68."

"…'course, Mama never liked her," mused Harry. "Kept saying she was fast. Seemed like there wasn't anything Mavis could do right far as Mama was concerned."

"I see," said Gemma, waiting for more revelations, but he was quiet, head bowed over his coffee, seemingly sunk in reminiscences.

"So," she said, after a minute or two had passed. "Is there anything in particular that *you* think I should be working toward with St. Elwood's?"

"Well, if you ask me," said Harry "--which you have, of course – if you ask me, I think it's time we brought back the Snow Goose!"

Chapter 8

"Now mind you, said Harry, "I understand the Snow Goose isn't strictly a part of the worship service. But it was an important aspect of our role on the island, and the congregation hasn't really been the same since the Snow Goose died."

"So," said Gemma, "what exactly is – or was – the Snow Goose?"

"The Snow Goose was this big white van that the university gave Professor Lindquist when his wife lost her foot to diabetes," said Harry. "You know, one of the kind that had the lift in the back for wheelchairs? For distinguished service and all."

"And is Professor Lindquist a member of St. Elwood's?" asked Gemma.

"Oh, no. Him being a scientist and all, he don't hold with all this religion truck. Besides, as he says, "what kind of God would take away the foot from a sweet woman like Berit Lindquist, a true believer if there ever was one. And then give her cancer, too," added Harry.

"The Professor took it hard, he did, when Berit took sick. And after she died he took back the keys to the van and locked it in his garage. It's been there at least three years now, since before Father Parkinson took over."

"I'm sorry," said Gemma, "I don't understand. What does Professor Lindquist's white van have to do with St. Elwood's?"

"Well, when the U gave the van to the professor, they got one with lots of extra seats in it; I don't know, got it on sale or something. So one year, in January, Berit talked the Professor into letting the church use the van for a photo excursion to the Skagit Valley. You know, to photograph the snow geese when they take over the tulip fields? And that trip worked out so well that we began using the van for other excursions.

"Eventually we just made it a regular feature, doing weekly runs to the mainland as a service; you know, for groceries, and trips to the beauty parlor, and doctor visits and Costco and all. Pretty soon the whole town was using the thing. Joyce would keep track of the orders, we'd give rides to anyone who needed 'em, and the folks on the Goose committee would take turns driving the van and picking up all the stuff folks had ordered. We'd make the Thursday morning red-eye and be back in time for dinner, which 'ud be a potluck at the church. Whichever committee members weren't going into town would cook up a big pot of spaghetti, folks would come to the church, pick up their stuff and stay for dinner."

"Goodness," said Gemma. "It sounds like quite a complex undertaking."

"Oh, well, Berit, she kinda got everyone all organized and fired up about it, and with Joyce tracking the orders it seemed to work out real well. My Mavis, she wasn't much of a cook, but she loved driving in the van and talking with everybody. But with Berit gone and the van locked up there didn't seem to be any way to make it happen again. There's lots of people still in the habit of Thursday runs to the mainland. But now they all mostly take their own cars."

"And they pretty much stay in them, too," Harry added. "Used to be we'd all go up to the top level of the ferry, play cards and whatnot, maybe even sing sometimes. We'd always be caroling at Christmastime; got to be quite the tradition. But now folks don't even talk to each other anymore. And there's no more potluck suppers, neither."

"I see," said Gemma. "Perhaps I could talk with Professor Lindquist, see if he'd be willing to share the van again?"

"Oh, folks tried," sighed Harry. "But he weren't having none of it. 'Dead, she is, and dead she'll stay,' he'd say if anyone asked. "Dead she is, and dead she'll stay.' Couldn't tell if he was talking 'bout Berit or the van, but by the time you got the nerve to ask he'd slam the door in your face."

"I see," said Gemma. "When's the last time anyone spoke with the Professor?"

"I'm not sure," replied Harry. "I know they've got some woman from the County comes over once a week to bring him food and stuff. But he don't get out much since he got laid up with his hip."

"Hmm," said Gemma. "And what about that dog of his?'"

"Oh, that one's a menace," said Harry. "That's a big piece of why no one goes by there much anymore. Dog won't let 'em on the lot, stands there growling."

"Well that dog stole a sandwich from my little friend Jasper the other day," said Gemma. "I've been meaning to talk to Professor Lindquist about that. Perhaps as the new vicar in town I could pay him a social call…"

"Well, good luck to ya," said Harry. "But I doubt you'll get past the door."

"… well, thanks for the coffee," he added. "I better get home, chop some more wood before those cold winds return."

"Okay, Harry," said Gemma, pulling on her coat. "You be careful out there."

Gemma left a tip for their waitress, a sullen teen with a nose ring and hair the same unearthly shade of black as Joyce, their church secretary, then left Jonie's and headed back to her car. She stopped by the store and picked up some boneless chicken and a handful of mushrooms, then headed back up the long winding road to her cabin, thinking of the Professor, his dog, his wife and the Snow Goose.

Distracted, she almost didn't notice the family of otters crossing the road at the Neck, but fortunately she slowed down in time, just missing the littlest one as it lumbered across the road after its mother. *Otters*, she thought. *How cool is that? I wonder where they hole up at night…*

Gemma pulled into the driveway and smiled; Venice was sitting impatiently in the window, awaiting her return. *Old habits die hard, I guess,* thought Gemma as she threw her coat on the makeshift driftwood coatrack by the door and picked up the purring cat. Sundays they'd taken to sitting in the living room for a bit after church, talking about the service and the sermon, sharing gossip and raising concerns. It was one of Venice's favorite times, for Gemma was rarely still otherwise, and he'd spend most of their Sunday chat kneading her chest and licking her neck, chin, and hands – anywhere he could find a spare bit of skin.

"Okay, boy," said Gemma. "There's no one else to talk with, so I guess I'll just tell you." And she proceeded to fill him in on the morning's activities.

CHAPTER 9

That evening, after making herself a pasta dish with chicken, mushrooms, cream and sherry, Gemma retired to her bedroom and seated herself at her laptop, which sat invitingly at the little desk by the sliding glass door that led onto her deck. The clouds had lifted during the afternoon, and the moon had risen, almost full, sending a ribbon of light across the water from the islands beyond.

Venice lay curled on his fleece pad behind the screen, purring softly to himself as Gemma checked her email and began composing her weekly note to Alex. She told him the stories of Father Parkinson, the lodge and the RV, described proudly her flash of genius about the parish video, and shared the surprising tale of the Snow Goose.

"I'd been meaning to see Professor Lindquist anyway," she wrote, "because of the problems his dog is causing Jasper, the little boy whose mom studies massage therapy on the mainland. But now I'm thinking we need a different approach altogether. Did you ever meet him while you were on the faculty at the U? Or hear anything about him? He must be very bitter about his wife's death, to have so cut himself off from the town…

"Anyway," she continued, "do take care of yourself. I keep reading these stories about the super-viruses that thrive in hospital environments, and I know the sanitary conditions there are not the best. Please be careful."

Her notes to the girls were briefer and more upbeat – the girls were both worried about leaving her alone for a year, and seemed to need frequent reassurance that she could exist without them, so she kept things light and cheery.

Gemma had almost signed off for the night when she decided to look up Dr. Lindquist on the Internet. She began with Wikipedia and was surprised to discover a rather lengthy entry for him. Apparently he had worked under Einstein as well as on the Manhattan Project, and had come to the U at the end of his career, serving as an Esteemed Fellow to their physics department and holding the Olmstead chair until his retirement in 2001.

Gemma suspected Lindquist's decision to retire might have been at least partially motivated by his wife's struggles with diabetes. No mention was made of the gift of the Snow Goose, but it was likely the van had been originally donated while he was still living in the U District.

Einstein, eh, thought Gemma. Wasn't he a religious man? Perhaps there might be some connection there, some way she could use Einstein to reach out to him. *But first,* she thought, *I'll deal with the dog. Let's see what comes of that.*

On Monday, Gemma's day off, Venice woke her at 6 am. After letting him out she snuggled back under the warm covers and dozed contentedly until the phone rang just before 9. It was Joyce, at the church.

"I'm sorry," said Joyce. "I know I'm not supposed to bother you at home. But there seems to be something wrong with the septic system here at the church, and there's the most awful smell…"

"Oh, dear," said Gemma. "Do you know when the tank was pumped last?"

"Oh, no," said Joyce. "Well, at least, it hasn't been pumped since I came to work here, and that must be close to 5 years now. I thought we were on the town sewer; it never occurred to me to pump anything."

"Well, see if you can find any records of either a pumping or a sewer bill. If we are on the town sewer, they should be sending us regular bills; you don't get services like that for nothing."

"I'll give Harry a call, then," said Joyce, "he's the church treasurer, you know."

"I see," said Gemma. "Is there anything Harry *doesn't* do?"

"Sleep with his wife," said Joyce with a giggle, and then she apologized. "I'm sorry, ma'am, it just slipped out."

"Well it wasn't very nice then, was it," said Gemma irritably. *What was it with small towns,* she wondered, *that everyone's sex life was everyone else's business.* And then she realized she was just grumpy about being awakened.

"Anyway," she continued, "please do give Harry a call. And if it turns out to be septic, just go ahead and call the local pumper; tell him it's an emergency," said Gemma. She was tempted to crawl back under the covers, but Venice was scratching impatiently at the sliding glass door, so she let him in and headed for the kitchen to roust up some coffee and plan her day.

Laundry, for sure, she thought, making a note on one of the 3x5 cards she kept for list-making. *And I should probably get some flashlights and candles... a couple of big jugs of water... move the wood out by the driveway closer to the house... and I'll need to stop by Professor Lindquist's. I wonder if I should call first? Nah, better not,* she thought. *If I just show up there's a better chance I'll get to see what a normal interaction is like with that dog of his.*

Gemma put her mug in the sink and rinsed it out, then went back to the little bathroom at the end of the hall off her bedroom, hung up her robe, and brushed her teeth. Grabbing her clothes out of the hamper, she headed downstairs and threw them in the washing machine with what was left of the landlord's detergent, then went upstairs to add "detergent" to her shopping list.

Stepping out of her sweats, she donned a warm pair of flannel-lined jeans and Alex's old Patagonia fleece, sniffing it briefly to breathe in its Alex-scented musky fragrance. She stood by the door a minute, transported by the scent and staring unseeing out the window at the driveway beyond, thinking of Alex in India, and of the many times he'd wrapped his arms around her while wearing this very jacket.

A sudden movement in the driveway caught her eye, and she awoke from her reverie to see a deer go leaping off through the salal beside the cabin. *I wonder what Venice will make of that,* she thought, and grabbing her purse she set out for town. First stop, Professor Lindquist, she decided. Best to get that one launched as soon as possible.

CHAPTER 10

Professor Lindquist's house was easy to find; it was a lovely red-shingled farmhouse up on a hill across from the road leading to the island's elementary school. There was a loosely constructed cedar fence surrounding the property, and a worn notice at the bottom of the driveway declared "Private Property, No Soliciting Allowed." Not sure that there would be parking at the top of the hill, or what her car's reception might be, Gemma elected to park in the lot that served the little mall next door. Though the print shop and the chiropractor's office were open, the various and sundry sellers of New Age gifts and physics that occupied the rest of the shops wouldn't be opening for another hour; she doubted they'd object if she left her car there for a bit.

The professor's dog was nowhere to be seen as she walked up the drive, but she could hear barking emanating from within the house as she approached. The barking escalated in both frequency and volume when she rang the doorbell, but it seemed a rather long wait before she heard slow footsteps and the turning of the lock.

When the door opened, Gemma saw a stooped man with flyaway white hair restraining a large mastiff with some difficulty. The dog was straining against his collar, fangs bared and growling furiously. The professor made no apology for the obvious ill-temper of his dog, nor did he remonstrate with the animal, but stood looking up at Gemma with both hands on the dog's collar, as if to say, "Speak quickly and it had better be good."

"Professor Lindquist?" asked Gemma.

"Yes, that's me," he replied. His voice was surprisingly deep for so small a man, and the accent would have totally charmed Gemma had his tone not been so forbidding.

"I'm sorry to bother you. I'm Gemma Benson, the new interim at St. Elwood's."

"I have no time for religion," said Dr. Lindquist, and he began to nudge the door shut with his foot, pulling the dog back out of the opening as its growl intensified.

Gemma grabbed the door and pulled back. "I'm not here for your soul, Professor Lindquist," she said. "I'm here about your dog. He's terrorizing some of the children who have to walk this way home from school."

"Well come in, then. You'll see, he's not as bad as he appears," said the Professor, grudgingly opening the door wider but keeping a firm hold on the dog.

Gemma sidled in the door, keeping her distance from the still-snarling beast. The professor motioned her through a doorway into a surprisingly tidy sitting room, furnished with a pleasing collection of Swedish modern pieces.

"Sit," said the professor, and, misunderstanding him, Gemma dropped into the nearest chair. "Not, you," said the professor, "the dog."

"Gunnar, sit," he said again, and the dog obediently dropped onto his haunches, eyeing Gemma with obvious distrust.

"Shake, Gunnar," said the professor, but instead of putting out his paw the dog rose and began shaking his whole body as if he had just been swimming. Gemma felt herself starting to giggle, and, looking at the professor, saw a twinkle in his eye.

"Greet, Gunnar," said the professor, and the dog obediently came to where Gemma sat torn between giggling and cowering. Gunnar sat directly in front of Gemma, looked her in the eye, and offered his paw.

"Well, hello there, big guy," said Gemma. "That's quite a show you put on for me." Gunnar wagged his tail enthusiastically, then leaped suddenly to his feet, braced his front paws on the arms of Gemma's chair and began enthusiastically licking her face.

"Gunnar, DOWN," shouted the professor, and the dog dropped to the floor, noisily licking his lips.

"I'm sorry, he's young yet and doesn't quite know his manners," said the professor. "Now, what's this about terrorizing the youngsters?"

"There's a young boy in town, Jasper? You might know him. He lives with his mother, but she's getting a degree in massage therapy on the mainland, so Jasper's on his own two nights a week.

"Last weekend the key to their house went missing and we found Jasper bedding down in the church. I took him home with me, and when I offered to feed him it turned out he hadn't eaten since breakfast because your dog stole his lunch on the way to school."

"What day was that?" asked the professor.

"Friday," said Gemma.

"Ah, yes, my housekeeper comes Fridays; I go in to the U to get out of her way. She did leave a note saying the dog had gotten out for a bit. I am sorry, we do our best to keep him in or on a leash but he has rather a lot of energy and it's sometimes difficult to contain him."

"Perhaps you should have named him Nuclear instead of Gunnar," said Gemma.

"Hmm." Said the professor. "I see you are as clever as you are religious."

"Well," said Gemma, "I don't actually consider myself very religious."

"You're not one of those spiritualists, are you?" asked the professor. "I may not have much truck with the church, but it's certainly better than all that new-age crap they sell in the stores down there," he added. "Crystals and what-not. They're right about energy, of course, but they won't find it in their damn Chakras."

"Ah," said Gemma. "I take it you don't agree with Einstein, then, that "all religions, arts and sciences are branches of the same tree."

"Who are you, anyway, Gemma Benson, to come into my home spouting Einstein? Certainly not the same brand of priest as that fool Parkinson."

"Well, thank you, I think," said Gemma, "though I've never met the fool myself. I've just been sent by the bishop to clean up the mess he left behind."

"Well you can start by kicking that Marcia Breezley out of the church," grumbled the Professor. "She made my Berit's life hell, she did; wouldn't be surprised if she didn't push her into an early grave."

"Really," said Gemma. "Well, I've only known her a few days, but I could certainly see how you might find her irritating."

"Irritating?" shouted the professor, and Gunnar leapt from his position on the floor and ran to the door barking.

"The woman is a damned nuisance. Gunnar! Stop that barking!" shouted the professor. "Gunnar, come! Now SIT!" And the dog obediently perched beside the Professor's chair.

"That Breezley woman wants to control everything in sight," grumbled the professor. "It's no wonder poor Orville spends most of his time sleeping; probably can't stomach the bitch when he's awake."

The professor looked sideways at Gemma to see if she would object to his language, but she kept a determinedly straight face and focused on Gunnar.

"Hmph," said the Professor.

"Well," said Gemma. "I guess that's all I needed to say. I did wonder, though, if I might bring Jasper by some day after school to meet your nuclear dog. It might help him over his fears."

"Hmph," said the Professor.

"Tell you what," said Gemma. "I'll give you a call when I figure out what time might work for Jasper and me. Thanks for listening, and hold onto that dog of yours!"

Gemma rose and motioned the professor to stay in his chair. "That's okay," she said. "I'll see myself out."

"Hmph," said the professor, and Gunnar growled softly as Gemma left the room and the house behind.

CHAPTER 11

Having bearded Dr. Lindquist in his den, Gemma's next stop was the grocery store which served Brandon's Rock. After a week of rushed visits to pick up essentials, she'd grown used to the collection of old codgers who gathered at the chairs and tables by the deli entrance in the morning to reminisce.

With a nod to the codgers, she grabbed one of the store's high wheeled baskets and began a slow circuit up and down the aisles. The store was surprisingly well-stocked for such a small town, and she was impressed with the produce section, where she stopped to grab a couple of salad bags.

Whatever did we do before salad bags? wondered Gemma, remembering the bother of being assigned before every meal as a child to the chore of washing and tearing lettuce. As she tested the avocadoes and found one that had just the right amount of give she found herself wondering -- *what ever happened to lettuce crispers?*

Some tomatoes, mushrooms, garlic, carrots, a green pepper, oranges and a bag of onions joined the avocado and salad bags in her cart, and she headed for the catfood. Thank heaven they stocked Venice's favorite brand, she thought, taking one of the larger bags and setting it on the bottom shelf of the grocery cart. She added a multi-pack of chicken breasts, a pound of ground beef, two cans of tomato soup, a box of whole wheat pasta, a bag of lentils, and a box of eggs to the cart, then found the batteries and flashlights in the aisle with the detergent and the gallon water jugs.

Hoping to find some of the dried banana chips she loved to snack on, Gemma backed up to the front of the store to look at the signs overhead delineating the contents of the aisles.

"Dried Fruit and Feminine Hygiene" read the sign over Aisle 13, and she pushed the cart in that direction, visualizing with a grin what Alex would say about that interesting combination when she wrote him next.

Standing in line at the checkout stand, Gemma gazed unseeing at the lurid headlines on the various tabloids and fan magazines displayed there as she mentally went through the rest of the day's list. "Excuse me?" said a brusque voice behind her. "Aren't you the new vicar of St. Aidan's?"

Emma turned to see a small elderly woman standing behind her, clutching her pocketbook and pushing a cart full of frozen dinners. "Yes," said Gemma, "I'm the new interim. And you are?"

"Eleanor Meacham," said the woman, holding out a gnarled hand for Gemma to shake. Gemma took it gingerly, but Eleanor's shake was surprisingly firm. "I hear the septic system's already started acting up," said Eleanor knowledgeably. "If you take my advice, you'll get the church back on a regular pumping schedule for that tank. The budget got so thin while Father Parkinson was here that the old fool thought that could easily be cut – anything but those crates of "communion wine" he kept storing in the basement!" she added.

"Ah" said Gemma. "I take it you're an active member of St. Elwood's – or do you prefer to call it St. Aidan's?"

"Doesn't much matter *what* you call it, the place is still virtually empty on Sunday mornings. Although I guess you might be able to fix that for a bit," she said, eyeing Gemma speculatively. "A woman priest is something of a novelty; there'll probably be some curiosity seekers for a bit."

"Well," said Gemma. "Maybe we'll get lucky, and the curiosity seekers will find more than they thought they were looking for and decide to stay for a bit."

"Not unless you've made some pretty significant changes in that service," huffed Eleanor. "Which I doubt, as long as you've got that Marcia Breezley as your warden and her sister Agnes on the organ."

"Oh," said Gemma. "I didn't realize they were sisters."

"Well, half-sisters, really," said Eleanor. "Marcia's father, Albert, was the warden of St. Elwood's back in his day, married to Marcia's dried-up stick of a mother, who was actually Elwood Senior's grand-daughter. She was the choir director then; the church was more popular in those days, and we had a pretty strong choir; she ruled them with an iron fist, and Marcia's father, too. But he escaped for a bit, I guess, and pretty soon that little school teacher they'd hired for the first –to-fourth graders was pregnant.

"She left the island for a year or two, and Albert went back to his wife, but when she came back a couple years later with little Agnes in tow and a tale about a soldier who died in Viet Nam we could all do the math."

"Really," said Gemma.

"Oh yes," said Eleanor. "Plus it didn't help that Agnes was a dead ringer for Marcia, and followed her around everywhere like a little shadow."

"I see," said Gemma, who had finally come to the front of the line and begun unloading her cart onto the conveyor belt. "And you, Eleanor, are you still active in the church?"

Eleanor shook her head. "Nope, and I'm not gonna be until something changes around there. But then," she added, sizing Gemma up, "given who the bishop put in as interim, my guess is there'll be some changes happening pretty quick. Vestry meeting tomorrow, eh, girl? Planning to knock them over sideways, are you?"

"Well," said Gemma, counting out exact change from her overflowing change purse. "It's tricky. It's obvious some things need to happen. But I'd rather the changes come from them, not from me. If I just walk in there like Jesus in the temple with the moneychangers, flipping over all their carefully guarded tables, they're likely to turn on me, and that won't do anybody any good."

"Hmm. I suppose that's true," said Eleanor, loading her frozen goods onto the conveyor belt. "So what's your plan?"

Emma helped the checker load her bags into her cart and looked appraisingly at Eleanor. "You know… you seem surprisingly interested in this church you have no intention of attending. What would you say to a cup of coffee with your new vicar?"

"I guess I could manage that," said Eleanor. "Got to get these groceries home and into the freezer first."

"Me, too," said Gemma. "Shall we give ourselves an hour to get home and straightened out? Where would you like to meet?"

"There's a garden club luncheon at 1 at the senior center," said Eleanor, "so I have to come back into town anyway. How bout we say 11:30 at Ehe Pilings."

"What pilings?" asked Gemma, looking confusedly out the front window of the store, wondering if she was to bring a cup down to some dock or other.

"Haven't you found The Pilings yet?" asked Eleanor. "Well then, "she said. "This'll be just the ticket; I bet you've been missing lattes, haven't you."

"Oh," said Gemma, breathing a sigh of relief, "you have no idea. Tell me where; I'll even pick you up if you like."

"Nope, that's okay. Just meet me in the church parking lot at 11:30 and I'll walk you over."

"Okay," said Gemma. "I'll see you at 11:30," and she pushed the cart out into the parking lot and began loading the bags into the back of her Subaru. *Oh, thank God, coffee,* she murmured to herself, stuffing the last bag into the front seat and returning the cart to the stack by the front door of the store. *I can't wait!*

CHAPTER 12

The Pilings turned out to be tucked into an out-of-the-way corner back behind and below the convenience store that sat – conveniently – at the main intersection in town, about 4 doors down from the church. The little café was warm and busy, the air redolent with the scent of fresh-baked cookies and cheese croissants, their specialty. But the best smell of all was the coffee, and Gemma sipped hers enthusiastically, reveling in the familiar taste of her favorite coffee blend, a mocha breve.

"So, Eleanor," she said, after swallowing a bite of the largest and gooiest chocolate chip cookie she'd ever seen, "how is it that you know so much about St. Elwood's?"

"Well," said Eleanor, "we've actually had a place on the Rock since the 1930's, though we didn't officially move here 'til Bill retired from the Navy in '56. And my dad was an Episcopal priest, so it just sort of made sense to stay connected with the church here. My kids were acolytes growing up, and both our girls were married here. Bill and I sang in the choir for years, although that stopped when he got sick, and then of course I was too busy nursing him for the last two years.

"Once Bill and the kids were gone there wasn't that much to do here, so I began helping out at the church. Taught a little Sunday School, helped with communion… I was a lay reader for a while, an usher, a greeter; served on the Vestry for a bit, was a convention rep for 6 years straight and even got to go to the General Convention the year it was in Indianapolis. Now that was something! All those hundreds of people all in one room, all praying the Lord's Prayer in their native languages? Whew! Felt like the spirit was gonna lift us all right outta there!"

"And now?"

"Now I don't darken the damn door," said Eleanor. "Bad enough old Parkinson was down in the basement getting drunk and cavorting with that Mavis woman. But for the rest of them to put up with it; well I couldn't stand that. Man of the cloth or no man of the cloth, a priest is a child of God just like the rest of us. You don't discipline one child and not another, just because he wears his collar backwards.

"But he'd get up there at those AA meetings – and of course by this time half the vestry was in AA because no one else would agree to serve anymore – and confess to his sinfulness and they'd all get slain in the spirit or whatever and turn a blind eye to the fact that come Monday he'd be sleeping it off again."

"So Eleanor," said Gemma, breaking off a piece of cookie and offering it to her, "do you think you might consider coming back?"

"Can't rightly say," said Eleanor. "You seem nice enough, and I like you. But I'm not sure I'm willing to deal with all those folks that made such fools of themselves over Father Parkinson. Speaking of fools," she added, looking intently out the window, "there goes that Ronnie Breezley on his bike again. Off to Madrona Park to smoke weed with his buddies, probably."

"Breezley?" queried Gemma.

"Yup, that's Marcia's boy. Claims he's a house painter, but he seems to spend most of his time hanging out at the grange with his doper buddies."

"Really."

"Yup. Apple didn't fall that far from the tree, either; Orville may not be a stoner but he does like his alcohol. That's why he sleeps so much."

"So, um, speaking of alcohol," said Gemma, trying to steer the conversation back to church, "don't you miss communion sometimes, after all those years?" asked Gemma.

"Sure," said Eleanor with a sly grin, "but you can bring me communion; don't have to go to church to get it now, do I!"

"Hmm," said Gemma. "Could be my car develops a dead battery on Sunday afternoons – I know there are Sundays when I sure do!"

"Tell you what," she added. "Let's just say there's a communion cup in your future, and we'll see how it plays out."

"Fair enough," said Eleanor, rising slowly from her chair and carefully stretching out her knees. "For now I'd better get over to the senior center. Marcia Breezley's got a pumpkin competition going, and I've got one in my car I'm pretty sure will beat anything she could have come up with in that puny excuse for a garden she pokes around in."

"Do you need help carrying it in?" asked Gemma.

"Oh, no thanks. Professor Lindquist has a hydraulic cart he brings along to help with that sort of thing."

"The Professor is in the garden club?"

"Oh, yes," said Eleanor. "His specialty is roses, though, so he doesn't talk much this time of year. You should see the one he spliced together after Berit died. Prettiest peach color you ever saw. We're trying to get him to officially register it in Berit's name, but so far he's resisting. It's too bad, really; I don't think he's ever grieved properly for Berit, so of course he can't seem to get over the loss, either.

"Well, we all know it takes time to grieve," said Gemma, remembering her own sense of devastation and sorrow after the loss of her son. And she never had a chance to live with him. What must it be like to lose someone with whom you've been close for 30 years or more? It didn't bear thinking about, she decided, especially not with the rest of her immediate family scattered so far away.

"Here, why don't you let me get the door for you," she said, and they left the warm coziness of The Pilings, bracing themselves against the cold November wind.

Gemma waved at Eleanor as her new friend pulled out of the lot in her ancient and slightly dented blue Corolla, then headed across into the church office. "I take it the septic problem hasn't been solved yet," she said to Joyce, wrinkling her nose at the fetid smell emanating from the men's bathroom.

"I checked the records, and it's clear the vestry voted against tying in to the town sewer when it came through back in '92," said Joyce. "So I have a call in to the Urbizo brothers; Paulie runs a septic pumping business on the side when he's not helping Carlo with construction projects. I'm sure they'll get back to me before the end of the day – at least, I hope so. That Paulie, he may smell funny sometimes, but he sure is easy on the eyes."

"Well beauty is as beauty does," said Gemma. "I'll be happy to admire him but I'll be happier if he can get this smell out of my office. Good thing I'm working at home today!" she grinned. "Thanks for holding down the fort; I'll see you tomorrow?"

"Yup," said Joyce. "I'll be in a little late, because I'm supposed to meet with Darla's teacher at 9, but I'll be in after that."

"Oh, is there a problem with Darla?"

"I don't think so; she just said she needed me to come in..."

"Well, good luck with that," said Gemma. "I'll see you when you get back."

"Okay," said Joyce. "Take care, now!"

"You, too," said Gemma, and she closed the door behind her, took a deep appreciative sniff of the cool air blowing in off the Bay, and climbed into her car. *I wonder whose pumpkin will win,* she thought as she drove out the long hill that led to the other side of the island. *And how on earth am I going to get rid of my senior warden?*

CHAPTER 13

Once home, Gemma moved the laundry into the dryer and decided to tackle the wood. She found an old rusty wheelbarrow back behind the carport, and the wheel seemed to work reasonably well, so she donned a pair of fingerless gloves and wheeled the barrow out to the woodpile near the end of the driveway.

Filling the barrow with as much wood as she thought she could safely lift, she rolled it back to the dwindling woodpile outside the front door of the cabin. After repeating the trip several more times, assisted and occasionally hindered by Venice, she had pretty much restored the porch pile to the size it had been when she moved in, so she returned the barrow to the back of the carport, shook out her gloves, and left them by the front door.

The dryer was still churning downstairs, so she decided to stoke up the stove and curl up in one of the big chairs in the living room. She picked up her Bible, planning to take a look at the passages for the week, but somehow her heart wasn't in it.

Clearly it wasn't going to be enough to get the remaining people at St. Elwood's excited about a parish video. Or even to get them to consider playing different music on Sunday, or switching to Rite II (God forbid). They really needed to be turned inside out. Was she really the woman for the job?

Lulled by the warmth of the fire and the confusion of her thoughts, Gemma was beginning to drift off to sleep when the phone rang. Startled awake, she stumbled a bit trying to remember where the phone was, and finally answered after the third ring.

"Out beach-combing?" boomed the bishop's voice.

"Nope," Gemma replied, "I was actually dozing after bringing in the wood."

"Ah, the country life. How positively pastoral of you."

"Right," said Gemma. "Did you have a reason for this call, or did you just want to gloat?"

"Ah, Gemma, ever the suspicious one," replied the bishop. "But of course I do have a reason. I'm calling to see how you're planning to handle that vestry meeting tomorrow night."

"Actually," said Gemma, curling up in the chair again, "I haven't a clue."

"Well, you know what Einstein used to say, don't you?"

"No, what?"

"No problem can be solved from the same level of consciousness that created it."

"Are you trying to be helpful?" asked Gemma, "because, if you are, you're not being very successful. What exactly is it you're trying to tell me?"

"Well, first off," said the bishop, "do you know them well enough to understand how they think?"

"Can you ever know anyone that well?"

"Oh, now, don't go all theological on me, Gemma dear. I'm just saying you need to figure out what their level is, and then approach the issue from another level."

"Hmm," said Gemma. "I think I may have already begun that," and she told him about the parish video plan.

"Excellent," said the bishop. "Now if you can actually get people to watch those videos, I think you'll have something. But what's their incentive?"

"A deep desire to win?" asked Gemma.

"Not everyone has your competitive spirit, Gemma," said the bishop fondly. "I'm thinking food, shelter, clothing, pride… the basic motivational aspects of life. This sounds like a perfect venue for the venerable Parish Potluck."

"It sounds a bit pedestrian. Though I suppose I could suggest to Marcia that she organize it, which would get her out of my hair for a bit. And it would be an opportunity for parishioners to meet me and for me to meet them."

"And…"

"And," echoed Gemma, "another chance to step on the soapbox…"

"Well, might be a bit early for that," mused the bishop. "Best to start by staying focused on the original plan: that they'll produce a video for potential clergy, and find some sort of community ministry to promote. My guess is that you being a woman is quite change enough for them right now, and they'll be clinging mightily to whatever feels safe and familiar 'til they get over this initial hump. But I'll make sure the videos you get include some women clergy in more conservative parishes. Although... do we have any of those?"

"I believe that's your problem, not mine," said Gemma. "Speaking of women -- how are Margaret and the girls?"

"Excellent, excellent," said the bishop, and the rest of the conversation was spent comparing parenting notes.

The dryer buzzer rang just as the bishop hung up, and Gemma went downstairs to deal with the laundry. But when she opened the dryer door, the clothes were still wet: though the dryer had been rotating beautifully the heat seemed to have failed.

Apparently this was not the first time this had happened, as she found a length of clothesline tied to a hook over by the workbench. A quick scan found another hook in the opposite corner and a cloth bag filled with clothespins, so she set about hanging the wet clothes up to dry.

Back upstairs, she called the Urbizo brothers and left a message about the dryer; with any luck they weren't answering because they were off pumping the tank at the church...

Glancing at the clock, Gemma realized it was time to start thinking about dinner. She began browning beef, onions and peppers; a simple pot of spaghetti would give her leftovers for most of the week. Once the sauce and noodles were bubbling, she sat down at the kitchen table with a pad and paper and began drafting up an agenda for tomorrow's meeting.

By 9:00, she had eaten, the leftovers had been stored in single-serving containers, and she had a working agenda as well as an idea for a Bible study that might trigger some new thinking. The fire was dying down in the woodstove, so she flipped on the bed-warmer, threw on another log, turned the thermostat down, and slipped into her fleece pajamas. The landlords had left a motley collection of old Agatha Christie paperbacks in the shelf above the bed, so she turned off the bed-warmer, crawled under the covers, and read herself to sleep with an old Miss Marple novel. She was glad to tuck in early, as tomorrow would be a long day.

CHAPTER 14

Now that Gemma knew about The Pilings, she made a point of stopping in for a mocha breve before showing up at the church. The front and side doors of the church were both locked when she arrived; apparently Joyce was still meeting with Darla's teacher. Gemma let herself in, turned up the thermostat and stopped into the sanctuary for a quick prayer. *Not my will, but thine be done, O Lord*, she thought, but then she threw in a couple of her own suggestions for good measure. Gemma believed that God was always in charge, of course. But she was also a pragmatist and believed in asking for what you want.

Couldn't hurt, anyway, she thought, as she unlocked the door to her office. There was a flimsy blue bill on her desk; apparently Paulie Urbizo had managed to get the pumping done. She hoped they knew to call her here about the dryer; she made a mental note to call again that afternoon if she hadn't heard from them.

"Halloo-oo!" trilled Marcia. "Anybody home?"

"In my office," called Gemma, and mentally girded herself for whatever battles lay ahead.

"You'll need a few puffs of that air freshener to get rid of the septic odor in here," Mrs. Breezley observed as she sailed in and moored herself into Emma's armchair. "I've brought the agenda for tonight's meeting," she added, waving a sheaf of papers. "You'll need to get Joyce to Xerox them of course. 11 copies, I believe; I'll have my own of course."

"Actually," said Gemma, "I…

"…And I've made an appointment with Carlo Urbizo to get estimates on the kitchen and the roof," added Marcia. "I'll be meeting him here at three, but of course you don't need to busy yourself with that; I'll take care of everything."

"Actually," said Gemma, "I…"

"Where *is* Joyce, anyway?" asked Mrs. Breezley, craning her head around the wing of the chair to eye the doorway, beyond which sat Joyce's desk. "I suppose that daughter of hers, that Darla, is sick again. If you ask me Joyce is way too indulgent with that child. Comes of being a single parent I guess, but in my day children had fathers as well as mothers and didn't stay home every time they got the sniffles. Why, my Ronnie had a perfect attendance record all through high school!"

Ah, thought Gemma. *And a lot of good that does him in his illustrious career as a part-time house painter. God knows what Ronnie does with the REST of his time*, she thought, but, having seen him tearing through Madrona Park on his mountain bike with his friends, she had a pretty good idea.

"I believe Joyce had a teacher's conference," she added aloud to Marcia.

"Well, that comes as no surprise; I'm sure it's not her first and I'm sure it won't be her last, either. Do you know what that child did this week?"

"No, I don't," said Gemma.

"She had the nerve to correct Mrs. Carleton's grammar!" sniffed Mrs. Breezley. "Pointed right to the blackboard, she did, and said 'You don't need an apostrophe with that its, Mrs. Carleton. It's a possessive, not a contraction' she goes, plain as day, and her only in 5th grade. What does a fifth grader know of possession anyway?" she asked.

The outer door slammed, and both women looked up as Joyce strode angrily into Gemma's office. "That *bitch*!" she said, not seeing Marcia in the wing chair in the corner. "She had the nerve to accuse Darla of insubordination! 'The child is disruptive' " she said in a singsong imitative voice. "Of course she's disruptive, goddammit," thundered Joyce, "because she's fucking bored out of her *mind*!"

Joyce turned to pace on Gemma's rug and noticed Mrs. Breezley huffing in the corner chair. "Oh, I'm sorry Mrs. Breezley, I didn't see you there."

"Never you mind about me, Joyce Finley. You should be watching your language around a woman of the cloth! And I wouldn't be so quick to blame Mrs. Carleton; that daughter of yours has been a pain in her side since that first day on the playground. What that child needs is some discipline, and if you can't provide it you could at least considering marrying someone who would!"

Joyce pursed her lips together, gave Gemma a speaking look, and turned to leave the office. When she neared the door, Marcia stood and waved her papers. "Oh, by the way, could you Xerox these for tonight's meeting dear?"

"In your dreams," said Joyce, and she stalked off to the sanctuary to have a good cry.

"Why don't you leave your agenda with me, Mrs. Breezley," said Gemma. "I'll see that we have what we need for tonight's meeting."

"All right," said Marcia. "But remember, it's her job, not yours, to see that those notes are copied. Oh, and I included the minutes of the last meeting as well; we'll need those copied, too," and she strode haughtily out of the room.

Curious, Gemma read through the agenda and minutes Marcia had left behind, then shook her head. *Oh, no*, she thought. *This will never do*. And she went to find Joyce to see if she could offer any comfort.

When she peered around the door into the sanctuary, she found Joyce huddled in one of the side pews, her arms wrapped around her knees and tears streaming down her cheeks.

Gemma slid into the pew beside Joyce and put a hand on her knee. "Tough day, huh?"

"It's just so hard," said Joyce. "It's bad enough having to do it all alone. But it's so much harder with a kid like Darla. She's not *like* the other kids, but she's so amazing, and no one seems to understand that here."

"She does seem amazingly bright for her age," said Gemma. "Have you had her tested?"

"Well, the school has," Joyce replied with a sniffle. "But all the testing people said was that she wasn't ADD – which I could have told them anyway," she said bitterly. "Darla doesn't have any problem staying focused. The problem is getting her to walk *away* from something she's focused on… and her social skills, of course. She just doesn't seem to get the other kids – plus, of course, her vocabulary is so far ahead of theirs they can't understand her half the time anyway."

"Hmm," said Gemma. "Sounds a lot like my Serena. Have you had Darla tested for Irlen Syndrome?"

"What's that?" asked Joyce.

"I'm not sure I can explain it very well," said Gemma. "But whatever it is, sometimes it causes reading disabilities – which Darla obviously doesn't have – and other times it seems to affect social abilities, with symptoms that sometimes resemble those of autism and ADD."

"But what good does it do to know *why* she's different?" asked Joyce. "I absolutely refuse to start giving Darla drugs!" she said fiercely, wiping her eyes.

"Actually, that's what's so cool about it," said Gemma. "The cure is just to wear a pair of colored glasses. I have a friend who has some sort of pinky-purple ones, and she says they make a huge difference. We ended up getting Irlen glasses for Serena; her lenses turned out to be a sort of orange color... The important thing is that a simple thing like colored glasses can make a huge difference. Tell you what: you should go look at the Irlen.com website. I'll write it down for you and you can check it out for yourself."

"Thanks, Gemma," said Joyce. "I'd like that. And thanks for listening; I'm sorry I broke down on you... I'm not sorry I insulted Mrs. Breezley, though – she had it coming! Now I just have to figure out how to get Darla out of Ms. Carleton's class ASAP, because this is not working!"

"Is there another 5th grade teacher?"

"No, but there's 4th – 5th combo team at the alternative school. I didn't want to send her there because her only friend goes to the regular elementary. And I'm worried she'll be too far ahead of her classmates if the teacher is teaching down to the 4th-graders. But I'm beginning to think I have no choice."

"Well, it sounds like you should definitely look into it. Come into my office, and I'll write down that website for you. And we should get busy running copies of the minutes and the agenda for tonight, though I think it'll have to be my agenda, not Marcia's. Why don't you start with the minutes, and I'll see if I can put together some compromise solution on the agendas. I don't want to upset too many applecarts, but I also have no intention of running the meeting like a dictatorship, with no prayer or Bible study.

"…and here's a Kleenex," she added, handing it to Joyce with the slip of paper on which she'd written the Irlen website address.

"Thanks," said Joyce, "I'll get right on that. And you did find the septic bill, right?"

"Yes," said Gemma. "I've put it in Harry's box, but thanks for running it by me. Clearly we're going to have to get back on some kind of regular schedule; their emergency charges are positively exorbitant."

"I agree," said Joyce. "Maybe you should add that to the agenda?"

"No," said Gemma, "I'm thinking we'll put that one off 'til we start looking at the budget. That's next month, right?"

"Yes," said Joyce. "But you're going to need to at least talk SOME about the budget tonight; there's going to be a pretty big shortfall, as there was no one here to run the stewardship campaign after Father P left. Lots of people aren't coming anymore anyway, and those that are still holding down the fort certainly haven't upped their pledges any."

"Not surprising," said Gemma. "You know, fundraising's not exactly my specialty… I wonder if Marcia has a gift for that? Hmmm – maybe I could put her on special assignment and put in a temporary warden to free her up for that. Although, maybe she'd just alienate everyone further and there'd be no money at all!"

"Actually," said Joyce, "I think you might be on to something. Marcia just loves to organize. Maybe if we gave her something important to organize on purpose she'd stop trying to organize everything else around here!"

"Okay, I'll see if I can work that into the meeting. That might also be a great excuse for not using her agenda; I can say I wanted to surprise her…"

"Works for me," said Joyce.

"Well, we'll just have to see if it works for her as well!" said Gemma, and she sat down at her desk to draft a schedule of topics for the evening.

CHAPTER 15

There was a festive mood in the Parish Hall as the vestry gathered for their first meeting with their new interim priest. Gemma had decided refreshments were in order, and had heated up some spiced cider and ordered pumpkin cake from The Pilings bakery.

Harry arrived early for the meeting, and shook his head morosely when he saw the Urbizo Brothers septic pumping bill. "That Paulie's been bugging me for months to let him pump the tank, and I keep telling him no. I hate it when people spend unauthorized money."

"We had no choice, Harry," said Gemma. "The tank backed up and overflowed into the men's room; I'm surprised you didn't notice the odor when you came in --it's still pretty strong."

"I get that," said Harry, "but I still don't know how the heck we're gonna pay for it."

"Well that's one of the things we'll be discussing tonight," said Gemma. "It's clear we're going to need some sort of major fundraiser to get through the end of the year, and I've got a couple of ideas I think you might like."

"What's that about a fundraiser?" asked Marcia as she strode into the hall.

"Oh, Marcia," lied Gemma, "just the person I wanted to see. I decided to make some changes in your agenda; I hope you don't mind. But I felt the fundraising was just so important that I wanted to get on that right away."

"It seems to me," said Marcia, gearing up for battle, "that..."

"Oh, hello," Gemma greeted an elderly couple who were peering tentatively around the door. "I'm Gemma Benson, your new interim vicar. And you are?

"George Wilcox," said the man, offering his hand.

"And I'm Doris Olivetti," said the woman. "We come together because we both live in the Island Center."

The Island Center, Gemma had learned, was a housing complex for the elderly, offering independent apartment living but communal cooking, a shared garden (which had apparently been the subject of many altercations), and a social hall with regular programs sponsored by the Senior Center.

"It's so nice to meet you," said Gemma, taking their hands and ignoring Marcia's sputtering off to the side. "Won't you come and have some cider and pumpkin cake before you sit down!"

"Why that's so nice," said Doris, "did you bake it yourself?"

"Oh, no, I picked it up from the Pilings bakery."

"Oh, wonderful," smiled George, "they're the best on the island."

"I'm so glad you approve," said Gemma. "Please, help yourself; and if you could fill out a nametag I'd be most grateful; my memory for names is just abysmal. If you'll excuse me, I see some other folks wandering in."

The rest of the people who came into the Hall were all parishioners she had met after church the previous Sunday. Gemma shook hands with each, inviting them to try the cider and pumpkin cake and to please put on a nametag.

After about 10 minutes of socializing, Gemma asked them all to sit in the circle of chairs she had drawn up in front of the rolling blackboard that was used for some of the Sunday School classes.

"How will we take notes?" asked Doris.

"Actually, Doris, how's your handwriting? If you're willing, I'd like you to keep notes on the blackboard behind me so we can all see what we've agreed on," Gemma said, making a quick decision and crossing her fingers that her usually effective snap judgment system hadn't failed her.

"I think I could do that," said Doris. "Long as I can sit when I'm not writing."

"I have an idea," said Gemma. "Harry, you're closest to the board, could you roll it over to stand behind Doris? Thanks," she said, and she smiled at her vestry members. "Thank you all for coming, and for being willing to try something new," she said.

"The last two churches I served did their worship in the round. I know that probably won't fly here – your sanctuary isn't set up for that, but I thought, at least for this meeting it would be nice to have that sense of openness and equality. And I thought maybe we'd just talk things over, instead of burying our heads in our notes. If you find it really uncomfortable, we can go back to the table for our next meeting.

"I thought that maybe as a little get-to-know-you exercise we might begin with a Bible study. I've set a Bible under each of your chairs, and I don't think any two people have the same translation. Our church library is surprisingly well stocked with a variety of translations; can anyone tell me who we have to thank for that?

"That was Berit's doing, that was, Berit Lindquist," said Doris.

"I see," said Gemma. "But she passed away a few years ago, I believe; has anyone been handling the library since then?"

"Oh, no, miss," said Flora, a fidgety little woman in an old fashioned shirtwaist and cardigan. "We've been keeping the library closed off to cut down on the heating bill."

"I see," said Gemma. "Well at least that explains why it's so cold in there! Okay then, let's begin. Our passage for this evening is Second Corinthians Chapter 9, verses 6 to 15. Who would like to read this for us? Thank you, Doris. And which translation are you reading?"

"The Good News Bible," said Doris.

"Great. Now, what I would like the rest of you to do while Doris reads is to follow along in your own translation, and note any significant differences you may find."

After a lengthy discussion comparing the different translations, Flora summed up the group's assessment of the passages.

"So basically," said Flora, "He's saying a stingy planter will get a stingy crop and a lavish planter will get an abundant crop. Everything we have is God's anyway, so if we give it away it's a way to thank God for his generosity – plus, the more you give, the more you get back."

Marcia, who had been growing increasingly restless, could contain herself no longer. "All this talk of giving has no bearing on why we're here tonight," she objected. "We can't even pay our own bills, let alone reach out into the community to help others. So I vote we stop this Bible study foolishness and get on with the business we came to conduct!"

"Actually, Marcia," said Doris rather tentatively, "I think this passage is totally relevant to why we're here tonight. Maybe if we hadn't abandoned our service to the community we wouldn't BE in this position. Maybe we shouldn't be so worried about paying our own bills but more about helping others and then somehow God will take care of us as well?"

"Puh," said Marcia. "Optimistic foolishness, that's what it is. Tell them, Harry. Dollars and cents are dollars and cents: if you don't watch them closely they slip away, and that's just how it is."

"I don't know," replied Harry. "What about the Parable of the Talents? Maybe we've been just burying our money. Maybe it's time to invest in the community for a change."

"Hmph," said Marcia. "Fat lot of good that's done us."

"Well," said Gemma. "We definitely have things to think about. Let's move on with the agenda and maybe we can begin to resolve some of these issues. Shall we begin by listing the challenges which face St. Elwood's at the moment? Doris, are you ready to write?"

"Yes," said Doris, grabbing her marker. "Let's get down to it."

CHAPTER 16

After her outburst following the Bible study, Marcia was somewhat subdued. Though she contributed quite a lot of useful information to the list of challenges that faced St. Elwood, she refused to participate in the priority setting exercise and sat with her arms crossed, radiating disapproval and occasionally rolling her eyes.

When Gemma got to the fundraising item on the agenda, however, she could see that Marcia was getting engaged as the various suggestions emerged. Some of the suggestions were the old standards – a bakesale, a movie night in the parish hall, a rummage sale – and, sticking to her ground rules about brainstorming, she insisted Doris write each one on the board.

"These are great – I can see you've all been thinking about this for a while. But we need something bigger," said Gemma.

"What if we were to revive the old Christmas Market?' said Shari. "If we expanded it we could do all three of those things, add in a craft sale, maybe a concert… Maybe we could even put together an auction of works from some of the local artists."

"Why would the artists want to donate their works to us?" asked George.

"What if half the proceeds went into the church funds and the other half went to revive the Snow Goose?" said Harry.

"But how would we do that?" asked Flora. "Professor Lindquist would never let us use that van again after what happened the last time."

"What happened to the van?" asked Gemma

"Oh," said Joyce quickly, "you don't want to know; it's another Father Parkinson debacle…"

"But surely," said Gemma, "surely we could…"

"I think," said Marcia, "that the only way we'll ever get that van back from Professor Lindquist is to offer him a fair price for it. And that's just one more bit of money we don't have."

"But sometimes," said Gemma, "you need to spend money to make money. If part of what we want to say in our video is that St. Elwood's works hard to meet the needs of this community, well, it seems to me from all I've heard that the Snow Goose was something that engaged almost everyone, and on a lot of different levels. Heck, we might even be able to get a grant for something like this, something that offers help to the aging, impoverished and housebound; reduces gas use and supports the local food bank."

"What if we break this down into manageable pieces?" she went on. "The Christmas Market would need an overall supervisor, and then maybe committees to be in charge of promotion, one to plan the bakesale, one to plan the rummage sale, one to be in charge of the entertainment – movie night, concert, or both – and one to handle the auction.

We'll need to figure out what percentage of the auction money goes to the Snow Goose and what percentage goes to the church, and I'm thinking we'll need one person to look at getting a grant to put the Snow Goose back in business. This would also probably be the perfect time to get some good video clips for the potential clergy; Harry, you said you could do the video, are you willing to do some shooting at the Market?"

"Let's wait and see if we need it," said Harry. "I think we have some scripting to do before we start randomly running around filming things."

"That sounds reasonable. Okay. Anyone interested in helping with that please talk with Harry after the meeting. Marcia," Gemma went on, "it seems to me that you're the best organizer we've got; would you be willing to be in charge of the Christmas Market? You have to agree to delegate to the other committees; we'll need you to be busy planning out the space and equipment requirements…"

"I'm not sure I can take that on right now, given all my work as Warden," said Marcia somewhat reluctantly.

Thank God, at last, Gemma thought to herself. "Well, what if you kept the title of Senior Warden but I found someone else to do the dirty work until after Christmas?" she asked.

"Well, who on earth would that be?" said Marcia, looking around the room at the other vestry members with some distaste.

"Actually," said Gemma, "you all remember Eleanor Meacham, right?"

"That woman hasn't set foot in this church in three years," said Marcia. "What's she got to do with this discussion?"

"Well," said Gemma, "I ran into her at the Market last week, and we had a terrific conversation. She's got a fabulous head on her shoulders, and I think she likes the idea of a woman priest, or at least of me," Gemma said modestly. "I know she's a bit reluctant to get back into the fray here, so to speak, but the Senior Warden is also known as the Priest's warden. They mostly only answer to and deal with the priest. So she could fill that role for a while, just 'til the Market is over, and then you could take it back."

"Hmph," said Marcia.

"Please," said Gemma. "I don't want to burn you out, and we really need someone with your gifts to run the Market."

"All right then," said Marcia. "I'll see if I can't put together a list of the duties she'll need to take over. It's only for two months, after all; she can't mess things up too much."

"Oh, Marcia, that's simply wonderful. How about a hand for Marcia as the chair of the new Christmas Market! All in favor, clap your hands!"

The vestry members clapped enthusiastically; some even cheered. Gemma led them in a closing prayer and then encouraged them to stay after and sign up and make recommendations for the various committees. There was so much excited conversation in the room that it was almost 11 before the last member left and Gemma was able to turn down the heat and the lights and head for home.

Driving the long road back to the cabin, she found herself murmuring repeated prayers of thanks – for the revelations of the Bible study, for the ideas and potential of the Christmas Market, for Marcia's willingness to step down, and a special prayer of gratitude for Eleanor Meacham – along with a prayer that she might say yes when Gemma called tomorrow morning.

She was also thrilled that Harry had signed up to do the grant research on the Snow Goose. He obviously had a lot of energy around the idea, and she was delighted to see him show enthusiasm after her original morose impression of him.

As Gemma neared home she noticed the wind was picking up, and a few white flakes were beginning to stick to the windshield. Snow! *Oh, dear*, she thought. *We have so little time between now and Christmas; I hope we can pull this off.*

Gemma let herself into the little cabin, hanging her coat and muffler on the makeshift driftwood rack by the door. Scooping Venice into her arms, she headed into the kitchen to pour some more dry food into his bowl.

"I know, I know" she said, putting him down only to have him meow impatiently at her. "I know I'm late, but it's all for a good cause. It was a good meeting, Venice, and I've got Marcia out of my hair for two whole months!"

Venice tossed his head, sniffed delicately at his food bowl, then walked into the bedroom, hopped on the bed and began washing himself.

"I know," said Gemma. "Believe me, I know. It's bedtime for me!" She turned on the bed warmer, threw one last log on the fire, pulled the drapes and crawled under the wonderful flannel comforter. "I'll definitely sleep well tonight," she said. "I'm so tired *nothing* will wake me!"

CHAPTER 17

Famous Last Words, thought Gemma at 2 a.m. as she sat huddled in her closet, wrapping her flannel comforter more tightly around her. The wind was roaring outside the cabin, and the surf was pounding on the rocks below. The power had gone out before she went to bed, but it was the thunderous sound of a large branch landing on the deck outside her bedroom that had sent her into the closet.

Judging by the Beaufort Scale the landlords had thoughtfully posted beside the door, the wind appeared to have reached gale force, and as she watched the sliding glass door bulge ominously with every new gust of wind, Gemma had decided discretion was the better part of valor. Taking her pillow and comforter into the long walk-in closet that led to the master bath, she shut the door behind her, but the wind was still whistling ominously through the cracks and the small space was cooling rapidly.

Gemma listened, her heart pounding, as the wind's volume continued to grow, and flinched every time yet another branch hit the house or the windows. What should she do if the doors broke, she wondered, alternating between devising an action plan and reassuring herself that the house had surely withstood other storms without damage.

Eventually she dozed off into a fitful sleep, waking with a start whenever there was a particularly large thump, and then sleeping again when her heart slowed back down.

By morning the wind's roar had quietened considerably. Gemma rose and stretched, then opened the door to see how the house had survived. The bedroom and living room looked just as they had when she had gone to bed the night before, but the big Adirondack chairs on the deck had all been slammed against the glass door. The wooden spool table was on its side, tucked into the corner of the deck and pinned in place by a dented crab pot with a red and white buoy hanging rakishly at its side.

All the bits of shells, beach glass, and driftwood that had been so charmingly arranged on the various surfaces of the deck had been blown away, replaced by windborne detritus – madrona berries, branches, pine cones and a generous coating of evergreen needles. A child's sneaker had lodged between the slats of one of the Adirondack chairs, and a dead seagull, its head twisted to one side, lay wedged under a large cedar branch.

Coffee, thought Gemma. *First things first; I'll get to the cleanup later.*

Fortunately the woodstove had a cook surface on top, so Gemma stoked up the dying fire, filled a pot with water and set it on the stove to boil. She had brought a small one-cup French press with her to use in case of just such emergencies, so she measured out a couple of scoops of her favorite roast, dressed warmly, returned the comforter to the bed, and sat down on the couch by the stove to wait.

A very long half hour later the house was filled with the scent of coffee and Gemma was munching on a cold croissant. Joyce had called to say the church had survived the windstorm unscathed but that several parishioners had stopped by to tell tales of damage and adventure.

"And that Jasper spent the night here again," added Joyce. "It was a good thing, though, as apparently the side door in the sanctuary wasn't properly latched and blew open during the night. Jasper was scared out of his wits when it happened, but he managed to get it closed before any damage was done."

"Oh dear," said Gemma. "I'm grateful, of course, but I hate to think of him having to spend the night at the church again. What on earth do you suppose his mother was thinking?"

"If you ask me," said Joyce, "she was probably out drinking with her buddies and just didn't bother to come home when the storm hit. Plus that trailer of theirs is so flimsy, Jasper probably felt safer here."

"Hmm," said Gemma. "Probably time to have a chat with his mom."

"Well, you're not going to have it today," said Joyce. "We've got a work party up here getting ready to go out and clear the roads; apparently there are several trees down between your place and town. Best to sit tight for now; do you have enough wood to stay warm?"

"Yep," said Gemma. "Speaking of which, I'd probably better go throw on another log. Call if there's any news."

"Will do," said Joyce. "Oh, and, by the way? I had a great idea for the Snow Goose project. Darla had a little toy van when she was a kid; looks a bit like the Snow Goose and opens from the top so you can put little people inside? How about if I find that – it's probably in one of her old toy boxes – paint it white, and put it out in the narthex with a sign to collect for the Snow Goose?"

"Sounds good," said Gemma. "Do you think you can get it out there by Sunday?"

"I'll do better than that," replied Joyce. "I'll get on it right away; take a look for it when I go home for lunch."

"Great," said Gemma. "It sounds like a perfect way to remind people of what we're about."

"Okay, then," said Joyce. "You take care of yourself out there – I'll check in again before the end of the day."

After finishing her coffee Gemma was restless, so she threw on her coat and muffler and went outside to tackle the mess on the deck. After she had straightened the chairs and the spool table, she threw the branches over the side to the woods below, swept off the berries, cedar needles and pine cones, and bagged up the gull and sneaker for the garbage. Climbing down the side stairs of the deck, she went around to the front of the house to put the bag in the garbage but the garbage can had apparently blown away.

Her car was safe, thank heaven, but one of the Doug firs by the carport had blown over, taking out the corner of the carport and effectively blocking the driveway. Gemma climbed over the downed trunk, leaving the bag by the car, and walked out the driveway to the road to assess further damage. She found an empty garbage can tipped over against the woodpile, but it wasn't one of hers so she righted it and dragged it out to the road for its owner to find.

Once out on the road, Gemma could hear the Blakely's generator going, so she wandered over to see if they might have spotted her garbage can. Commander Blakely was a retired Navy man with the passion for order common among that breed; he was out in his yard carefully piling burnable debris by his woodpile and running his chainsaw, cutting all the fallen wood into lengths that would fit into his fieldstone fireplace. Catching sight of Gemma, his wife June waved merrily from the kitchen window and beckoned her in.

"Have you seen my garbage can?" asked Gemma of the Commander as he stopped the saw to greet her.

"I'm not sure, but you might check down at the Neck," he said. "Things tend to collect there after a storm."

"Thanks," said Gemma, heading toward the house, where June now stood at the open door.

"Come on in, you poor dear," said June, "you must be exhausted. I bet you were up all night. That cabin is SO poorly insulated -- the wind must have been just screaming through. Can I offer you a fresh-baked oatmeal cookie?"

"Oh, thanks," said Gemma, "I'd love one."

"And how about some tea to wash it down?"

"Only if you have herbal, I think I've already had enough caffeine for one day," replied Gemma.

"Of course," smiled June. "We always keep herbal tea around for our girls. What is it with your younger generation? All us old folks can drink caffeine right up 'til bedtime, and you youngsters are hyperventilating after only a cup!"

"I don't know," said Gemma. "Maybe we're born pre-caffeinated cuz all our moms were so hyped up on the stuff," she grinned.

"Oh, you," said June. "Pre-caffeinated, that's good! I'll tell the Commander that one!"

"Got any cookies for me?' asked the Commander, poking his head through the front door. "I could sure use a break." He stepped in and dropped his carcoat on a tall wingback chair covered in a lemony chintz.

"She's a total slave-driver," he confided to Gemma. "She may be small, but she sure can crack the whip – she had me out there futzing with the generator as soon as the power went out. Pretty scary out there, all those branches blowing around, trees crashing in the woods…"

"Ah, but Herbert, you know you would have been miserable without the heat," said June fondly. "And your morning oatmeal!"

"Right," said the commander. "And, speaking of oatmeal, where'd you hide those cookies?"

"Right in front of your face, dear," said June. "What is it with men?" she asked, turning to Gemma. "They can't seem to find *any*thing without assistance!"

"I'm not sure it's just men," said Gemma. "My girls had the same problem. Amy particularly; that girl was *always* losing things."

"That's right," said the Commander. "It's not just the men. And besides," he said, settling into a large leather recliner by the fireplace, "who found the car in the parking lot at the airport the other day?"

"Ah," said June, "but that's cars. If it's got an engine in it, you know everything about it."

"And you don't," chuckled the Commander. "So, Gemma, how did you do in the storm – lose any windows?"

"Nope," said Gemma. "I spent the night holed up in that little hallway by the closets with the wind whistling under the door, but the house and my car are fortunately intact. The gutter on the corner of the garage roof got taken out by a tree, though, and the tree is blocking the driveway, so I'll not be heading into town anytime soon. I hear there's a work party going out from the church to clear the roads; I should probably give them a call to see if they can help me out when they're done."

"Oh, no need for that Gemma," said June. "Herbert loves an excuse to use his new chainsaw, and it looks like he's finished here. Herbert, dear, why don't you throw your coat back on and go help Gemma. Then maybe you can drive up the road and start clearing from this end."

"Splendid, splendid idea," said the Commander. "Well, Gemma, shall we go take care of that tree of yours?"

"Are you sure you want to do this, sir?" asked Gemma. "I don't have any urgent need to go to town…"

"No, no, no, it's perfectly all right," said the Commander. "Glad to be of service, Glad to be of service."

Gemma finished the last bite of cookie and followed the Commander out the door. "Thanks for the tea and cookies, June," she said. "Let me know if you need anything!" and she headed out the driveway with the commander and his chain saw.

"Do you mind if I take a run down to the neck? I'm determined to find that garbage can," confided Gemma.

"No problem," said the Commander, "I'll be finished here in no time."

"How about if I drive you up the road?" said Gemma. "Maybe there'll be other folks in need of help."

"Splendid," said the Commander. "Many hands make light work!" And he headed down Gemma's driveway while Gemma turned and went down to the Neck.

CHAPTER 18

So far the Neck was Gemma's favorite spot on Brandon's Rock. Her cabin was one of seven homes on Neck Point, a circle of land that was attached to the island by the Neck, a narrow two-lane road bordered on the south side by a row of beach pines and on the north by a rocky breakwater and a stretch of shallow beach. There was a beach on the south side as well, but it was separated from the road and trees by a small tidal lagoon filled with driftwood washed ashore by earlier storms.

She found her landlord's distinctive red plastic trashcan floating in the lagoon, fortunately close to the edge. She discovered that by holding on to one of the trees she could clamber just far enough down the bank to loop a long stick through one of the handles and pull; after a couple of false starts she was able to drag the can up and over a driftwood stump and onto the bank where she could grab it and pull it up onto the road.

"Ah, I see you were successful," said the Commander when she strode down the driveway dragging the can behind her. "I've got your tree all chopped up and stacked for you; be happy to help you split those logs later if you need it," he added. "Are you ready to head out?"

"Just let me dump this bag in the trash and get the lid on," said Gemma, "and then we can be on our way."

Gemma went in to pick up her keys while the Commander put his chainsaw in the back of her Subaru, and they headed out the Neck to see how the rest of the island had fared.

"Perhaps we should check on Eleanor Meacham," said the Commander, after they had cleared the first obstacle, a small poplar that was blocking the northbound lane. "Do you know if she has backup heat?"

"I'm assuming she does --" said Gemma, "—she's certainly been through enough winters here. But it certainly wouldn't hurt to be sure. I need to talk with her anyway."

The long driveway to Eleanor's home was surprisingly clear, but the path down to her cottage from the drive was completely blocked by an almost 6 foot span of roots from a cedar that had toppled in the storm.

"I can cut off this root system, but I don't want to risk my chainsaw trying to break it up," said the Commander. "We'll need to rig up something to drag it off the path. Do you have any rope in your car?"

"I don't think so," said Gemma, "but I think I can go around the other side of it to get to Eleanor's. Let me ask if she's got anything we can use – and be sure she's okay, of course. Why don't you check in that shed over there?"

Gemma thrust aside a motley collection of brush and brambles to get around the roots and back to the path on the other side. The remainder of the path was unobstructed, and she was relieved when Eleanor answered the door after the second knock.

"Why, Gemma, come on in, dear," said Eleanor as Gemma stepped into the toasty cottage. "You're covered in twigs and briars! Did you have to bushwhack to get here? How did you do in the storm?"

"Just fine," said Gemma. "I'm here with the Commander, who's been helping clear the road with his chainsaw. I'm afraid it's not enough to tackle the mess on your path, though; do you have a good stout rope we can use?"

"Yes, I saw the mess that downed cedar left up there; I've got a call in to Carlo Urbizo about that," said Eleanor.

"I doubt you'll want to wait until Carlo gets here," said Gemma. "I gather the roads are blocked in several places between here and town."

"Tell you what," said Eleanor, "just give me a minute; I think Bill had some nautical rope down in the crawlspace that we could use," and she disappeared into the kitchen. Gemma followed to find Eleanor lifting up a trap door in the laundry room closet. "There's a stool just below the opening," said Eleanor. "The rope should be on your left. I'm afraid I'm too old to get out again if I go down there, but here's a flashlight for you."

Gemma took the flashlight and lowered herself through the hole in the floor onto the stool below. The tide was in, so the sand below was covered with a couple of inches of water, but the rope was clearly visible on one of a row of hooks on a board to the left of the stool. Gemma lifted it off, handed the rope and flashlight up to Eleanor, then clambered back up off the stool and up onto the floor above.

"This should be perfect," said Gemma. "I'll go pass it to the Commander and we'll see if we can't clear some room for you to get out," she added.

"Here, I'll go with you," said Eleanor. "No use me twiddling my thumbs here while you do all the work."

"Thanks," said Gemma. "That'll give me a chance to ask you a favor."

"Uh-oh," said Eleanor. "Why don't I like the sound of this?"

"Remember how we discussed getting you into the church in a way a bit removed from the fray?"

"...yes..." said Eleanor slowly.

"Well Marcia has stepped down as senior warden for two months to run a fundraising project for us, and I wondered if you would be willing to fill in for her."

"Boy, you don't start small, do you," said Eleanor. "And this keeps me out of the fray how?"

"I'm hoping all the fraying will be around the fundraiser and that people's attention will be elsewhere," said Gemma, easing around the side of the trunk that blocked the path. "Here, let me hold this branch for you."

"Right," said Eleanor. "Dream on. And you're probably planning to completely redesign the service while the cat's away, eh, little mouse?" she said, stepping gingerly over a pile of brush.

"Guilty as charged," replied Gemma with a grin. "Well, maybe not completely. And I'm going to invite their input – after I show them some of the fun ways other churches do things...

"Right," said Eleanor as they approached the driveway where the Commander was tying a rope to the bumper. "Well, in for a penny, in for a pound. I don't think you'll succeed, of course, but I'll be happy to help you while you die trying!"

"Actually," said the Commander, "I've separated the trunk from the rest of the tree with the chainsaw, and I've cleared away all the obvious obstacles, so it should work just fine; no dying involved."

"Great," said Gemma. "With both of you clearing obstacles for me it should be smooth sailing from now on!"

"You wish," said Eleanor, and she rolled her eyes.

CHAPTER 19

By noon Gemma, the Commander, and Eleanor had made it all the way into town, having stopped a few times along the way in to lend assistance to fellow islanders in various difficult situations.

"I vote we have lunch," said Gemma.

"I second that," said Eleanor.

"Not for me, thanks," said the Commander. "June's been cooking up last night's potroast; she'd shoot me if I wasn't home for lunch."

"Oh, I'm sorry," said Gemma. "I'll run you back right away."

"No need," said the Commander. "I'll just catch a ride out with the Hawthornes. They mentioned they were going to go out to the Neck to check on their granddaughter."

"Are you sure?" asked Gemma.

"Absolutely," said the Commander. "Thanks for bringing me in."

"Thank *you* for helping me out," said Gemma. "Now go enjoy your potroast!"

"Yum," said Eleanor, "Potroast. Now there's something you don't eat much when you live alone."

"Yeah, me either," said Gemma. "Although my girls were vegetarians, so I didn't get pot roast much when they were around either. You know what?" said Gemma, turning to Eleanor, her eyes lit with anticipation.

"Oh, God, not another supper club," moaned Eleanor.

"No, really!" said Gemma. "This one could be different. Not church-related, for one thing – as I have a feeling we'll both need a break from church socializing. But what if it was just you and me and maybe I could ask Dr. Lindquist and Harry Borden…"

"Lindquist won't come and Harry's church," said Eleanor grumpily.

"But they're both living alone, and I bet they'd appreciate home cooking," said Gemma. "Truth is," she added, "I'd really like to invite Jasper, and this would be an excuse."

"Who's Jasper?"

"Jasper Morgan, that little boy whose mom studies massage on the mainland?"

"Oh, you mean that woman that has slept with every contractor on the island?"

"Oh, dear, really?"

"If Jasper's mom is Suzanne Whittaker, then, yes, really. I don't think anyone has any idea who Jasper's father is – probably why so many of the men are so nice to him," said Eleanor. "I think Andy Morgan took responsibility cuz he was married to her at the time, but of course he was a brute; thank heaven he's in Montana now.'

"Oh, dear," said Gemma.

"Well, I'll do it for Jasper," said Eleanor. "But I don't know how I feel about the other two. Probably doesn't matter, as I don't expect they'll agree. But now that I've got my mouth all hyped up for potroast, what say we head out to the Lakeside Grill? They do a real nice roast."

"Never been there," said Gemma.

"It's a bit of a drive," said Eleanor, "but you won't regret it, I promise. In fact, if either of us is ever too lazy to cook for this supper club of yours we could always order out from the Grill. Shari caters, you know."

"Shari? As in Shari Mattheson? On the vestry?"

"Yup," said Eleanor.

"We have a chef on our vestry? That's gotta be worth something," said Gemma as she turned onto the Deer Meadow Road, then swerved to avoid a large branch in her lane.

"Yeah, right – if you want to insist on giving the poor woman a busman's holiday," said Eleanor. "It's just another mile or so," she added.

"Oh, Eleanor, of course you're right. You're gonna be a great senior warden, you know; you know everyone and think of everything – just the sort of person I need."

"Hmph," said Eleanor. "I'm waiting to see what the vestry thinks of this idea."

"I already asked, and they seemed very open to it," said Gemma. "Except Marcia, of course. One of our primary goals for this next year is to begin bringing back all the folks who drifted away over Father Parkinson's antics. Who better to advise us on that than one of our most committed drifters?"

"Speaking of the Drifters, did I mention I heard them in concert a few years back?"

"Who are the Drifters?" asked Gemma.

"Whose idea was it to put a youngster like you in charge of this church anyway?" grinned Eleanor. "Turn left here; the grill is just down by the corner," and she began humming "This Magic Moment" under her breath.

The Lakeside Grill was a rather unprepossessing building – sort of a cross between a diner and a double wide – tucked under some cedars overlooking Meadow Lake. But the scent of home cooking that assailed Gemma's nostrils when she opened the glass door was definitely affecting her taste buds.

"Afternoon, Margaret," said Eleanor to the large red-haired woman who stood by the door. "Two for lunch please."

"Counter or booth?"

"Booth, please," said Eleanor. "These buns are getting too old to sit comfortably on those damn counter stools."

Lunch at the Grill lived up to its promise, and Gemma insisted on greeting Shari in her kitchen to thank her personally for the delicious roast.

"Wow," enthused Gemma. "Who knew you could get food like that on such a small island!"

"Yup," said Eleanor, "pretty fine. Don't think I'll need to eat again for a week at least; whatever possessed you to order pumpkin pie for dessert?"

"Just gearing up for Thanksgiving I guess," said Gemma. "Do we have time to stop by the church, or do you need to get home?"

"I'd better get back," said Eleanor. "I don't think I'm ready to set foot in the church yet."

"Okey doke," replied Gemma. "I'll get you home then; may I call Joyce from your place to see if she needs me for anything?"

"Mi telephono es su telephono," replied Eleanor. "Thank God for land lines; my nephew sent me a cellphone for Christmas last year but it only works two places on the island; I don't know what he thought I'd use it for."

"A camera maybe? That's about all they're good for up here."

Gemma pulled into Eleanor's drive and headed down the long hill, parking next to the stump they'd pulled from the path earlier. "How *are* you going to get rid of that thing?" she asked.

"Oh, I'll pass it off to one of the woodcarvers on the island," said Eleanor. "They're always looking for big pieces to make into kitsch for the tourists. Somebody's gonna be thrilled with it."

"Here," she added. "Make yourself at home. The phone's in the kitchen; I'm gonna head off to the little girl's room. Too many cups of coffee!"

Gemma dialed the church, and when Joyce answered Gemma asked if all the cleanup teams were back.

Joyce replied in the affirmative, then asked, "So did you get Eleanor to agree to be senior warden?"

"How did you know I planned to ask?"

"Island grapevine."

"But I didn't …"

"In this place, interrupted Joyce, "you just need to *think* it and everyone knows about it."

"I see," said Gemma. "Guess I'll have to be careful what I think – or think more quietly!"

"And don't I know it," said Joyce. "You take care now; no need to come back in. I'll see you tomorrow morning."

"Thanks, Joyce," replied Gemma. "But let me know if anything comes up, okay?"

"Sure thing," said Joyce, and Gemma hung up just as Eleanor came into the kitchen carrying a small mouse by the tail. She opened the door and tossed him outside, then came back in and began vigorously washing her hands at the kitchen sink.

"Don't know why I put them out," she grumbled. "This time of year they just sneak back in again when I'm not looking. At least it wasn't a rat."

"Ooh, there are rats?" asked Gemma, wrinkling her nose in disgust.

"Yup, the big Norway ones. You always run the risk of rats when you live this close to water. Rats and carpenter ants and salt spray on the windows. A small price to pay, if you ask me."

"Yes, well, I'd better go," said Gemma. "You take care, and thanks for everything."

"You, too," said Eleanor. "I'll be in touch."

Gemma waved goodbye and started up the path to her car. Time to begin planning Sunday's service: the parishioners of St. Elwood's needed a chance to hear some of the other possibilities in the world of liturgy. She planned to tap into the broader resources of the diocese, and had put the word out to her fellow clergy about contributing to Sunday's service adventure. But she'd have to be careful, she thought, as she slipped her key into the ignition. It's never a good idea to make too many changes too quickly. Best to keep things as they are for now and make it clear this was just an opportunity to sample other options.

CHAPTER 20

By Friday the rumor mill was working very efficiently. Word had gotten out about Gemma's choice of Eleanor, and with the exception of those who were secretly disappointed that they themselves had not been chosen, most of the parishioners felt it was a reasonable choice. After all, Eleanor was guaranteed to remember how things were "in the good old days," and would therefore presumably advocate only for those changes which would restore the church's former glory.

Everyone agreed change was afoot – anyone could see that with Marcia out of the way Gemma would be free to introduce whatever New Age or Popish Atrocities were out there. Would there be incense? Would Gemma sing the liturgy? Or, heaven forbid, bring in guitars? Most were feeling more curious than threatened, though many feared she might abandon the Rite I service altogether rather than return to the old pattern of Rite I at 8 and Rite II at 10.

So the usually peaceful sanctuary was abuzz just before 8 on Sunday morning as Gemma donned her alb in the sacristy. Harry, who already knew of Gemma's service plans, was calmly adjusting his cincture when Gemma tapped his shoulder. Together they bowed their heads in prayer, and then proceeded into the sanctuary. The room went completely silent, a deep hush awaiting her opening words.

"Please turn to page 323 in the Prayerbook," said Gemma. There was a quiet rustle of pages, and then a collective settling as Gemma began to speak the words of the traditional Rite I service.

"Blessed be God: Father, Son, and Holy Spirit," said Gemma.

"And blessed be his kingdom, now and for ever. Amen," replied her parishioners, and with those timeless words, the service was off and running.

After the benediction Gemma stood by the door, and she could feel the palpable relief of St. Aidan's Rite I regulars.

"You have a lovely reading voice," said an elderly woman in Irish tweed with a strong British accent.

"It's interesting, isn't it, how different the words sound when read by a woman," another, younger woman chimed in.

"They do, don't they," said Gemma. "Perhaps we should get together a discussion group sometime to talk about that."

"I hadn't thought about that part of having a woman priest," said one of the men. "It was intriguing. But it still feels wrong to have a woman heading up communion. I thought in the Eucharist the priest was supposed to be the body of Christ. And Christ sure wasn't a woman, or are you one of the ones that questions that, too?" he asked somewhat belligerently.

"Oh, no," said Gemma. "I believe Jesus was male. But the Body of Christ is the bread, not the priest. That's the point – you eat the bread, and you, the people, become the living body of Christ.

"Puh," said a short dapper gentleman in a goatee and a Greek fisherman's cap. "It's all Greek to me – or should I say, Aramaic?"

Gemma smiled. "Probably a little bit of both, I'd guess!" She said. "But it sounds like you might be a bit of a scholar?"

"Oh, I used to think I might go to divinity school," he responded. "Father Marino used to say I had the heart of a priest and the mind of a scholar. But then of course Father Parkinson came, and he had no patience with lay people who had ideas."

"Hmmm," said Gemma, shrugging out of her robe as the last parishioner walked out the door, leaving her alone with the dapper gentleman. "Sounds like I should get to know you better. What's your name?

"Chandler Ferris."

"Nice to meet you, Mr. Ferris," said Gemma, holding out her hand. "Are you ever available for coffee?"

"I work days in Friday Harbor, so it's hard to get away."

"How about in the evenings," said Gemma. "Can you break away? Or do you have a family you need to tend… "

"Actually, I live alone," he replied, "so I tend to work late and then just grab a quick bite in town."

"Could we maybe do that together some night?" asked Gemma.

"I think that would be okay," he replied cautiously.

"Great! What night would work best for you?"

"Well, Thursday's choir practice... how about Wednesday?"

"Perfect," said Gemma. "Where shall we eat?"

"How about SlaBonta – are you an aficionado of Mexican food?"

"I love Mexican food," said Gemma, "but what's SlaBonta? It sounds more like a Hungarian restaurant."

"Oh, sorry," Ferris laughed. "It's Isla Bonita, that place right on main street? Their letters – the I's – burned out a few years back and we just got in the habit of calling it SlaBonta..."

"Too cute," said Gemma. "Ok; I'm up for Sla Bonta on Wednesday – what time do you get back to the island?"

"How 'bout we say 6:30 – will that be a workable time for you?"

"Great," said Gemma. "See you then."

She turned and headed back into the sacristy, where Harry was just shrugging out of his cassock.

"So that went well, don't you think?" asked Gemma.

"Yup," said Harry. "But I think your sermon went right over their heads – either that or they just weren't listening."

"What makes you say that?" asked Gemma.

"Well, there was all that talk after the service about you bein' a woman an' all and not one person mentioned the actual sermon."

"Doesn't mean they didn't hear it," said Gemma. "Sometimes you plant the seeds and they don't sprout right away, they kind of crop up later."

"Well I hate to think what will happen when *these* seeds crop up," said Harry.

"Why," said Gemma, "what was wrong with the sermon?"

"Well, you know how the passage for today was about having compassion on the prisoners, and you kind of blew that out to encompass the whole mission field of people who are imprisoned by poverty and war and lack of education?" said Harry.

"Yes," said Gemma.

"Well that's not gonna fly too well with some folks around here," said Harry.

"Why not?" asked Gemma.

"Oh, I guess you really didn't know."

"Know what?"

"You know the Elwood this church is named after?"

"Yes."

"Turns out he died in the mission field, trying to convert the heathens."

"So?"

"It's in the constitution of the church: if we in any way support or encourage any mission work beyond this island the church building reverts back to the Bartenstein family."

"Oh. My. God. You have got to be kidding me," said Gemma. "Is that legal?"

"Whether it is or it's not, it's what people believe. So you preaching a sermon on serving those beyond our borders is pushing things a bit. Case could be made for you breaking the covenant with the Bartenstein will."

"Damn," said Gemma. "I was just trying to set the stage for a push to get the Snow Goose back; I wasn't even thinking about mission fields beyond the island."

"Maybe it's time you did," said Harry. "Stands to reason someone oughta challenge that will, doesn't it?"

"Oh, God, Harry; shouldn't we let sleeping dogs lie? There's already so much on the church's plate…"

"Afraid to put your money where your mouth is?" asked Harry. "What do you care anyway; it's not your church, it's just a place you're working for a year."

"Harry! That's a pretty bitter remark!"

"Sorry. Just gets me riled up, ol' Elwood reaching out from beyond the grave to stop our kids from going to Tijuana to build houses, or off to India like your husband."

"Well, Alex isn't in a mission field; he's just working in a hospital."

"You telling me he doesn't talk about what he believes? He's married to *you*, isn't he?"

"Wait – does this mean you think they could shut the church down just because of my connection to Alex?"

"Don't know," said Harry, "but if I were you, I'd stay on Marcia's good side."

"Why?"

"Cuz she's ol' Elwood's great-granddaughter, that's why. They close the church down for breach of covenant and she gets it. Been wanting to turn it into one a them community theaters for years," said Harry.

"Shit," said Gemma. "Shit, Shit, SHIT!"

CHAPTER 21

With only half an hour before the next service was slated to begin, there was no time for Gemma to rewrite her sermon. And, the rumor mill being what it was, she figured even if she rewrote it the news would get out about what she had preached at the early service. What to do, what to do…

In the end, Gemma decided to wing it. She vaguely remembered something in today's psalm that had struck her, but there wasn't time to look; she had to get vested. *Dear God*, she prayed as they waited for Agnes to strike up the opening hymn, *I need your help here. I've made enough other changes to this service to be noticeable (though not the hymns yet,* she thought, as Rock of Ages began its lugubrious march in the sanctuary); *please give me a sermon that will ease the transition and help them to trust me.*

Having processed behind Darla and Harry to the front of the church, Gemma turned to the congregation and said, "Good Morning."

"Good morning," they obediently replied, still standing.

"Please be seated," said Gemma. "As you know, I'm Gemma Benson, and I'm your interim pastor. As an interim," she went on, "I get to serve and preach in a lot of different congregations around the Diocese. And it turns out that each congregation has a different style of worship."

"Now, as many of you also know, we at St. Elwood's will begin putting together a video of our worship service to be shown to potential clergy. In preparation for that, several of us will be spending the next week or two watching similar videos that have been prepared by other congregations.

"But I thought that might not be fair, that only some people get to see how other churches do worship. So today, as a way of both introducing myself and sharing some of what I've seen around the Diocese, I have prepared a service which, though it has your usual music and the basic structure of your familiar service, also has ingredients from other churches around the diocese.

"Now, if I were really going to give you a taste of our churches, I would have started today's service by having Darla, our acolyte, swinging a censer of incense as she walked in, the way they do at St. Paul's in Queen Anne. But frankly," she grinned, "the one time I took my daughter there she began sneezing so at the incense we had to leave! So on the off chance that others of you might be allergic to incense, I have decided to dispense with that.

"But," she said, "St. Paul's was kind enough to loan us some of their vestments and an empty censer, so you can see what it looks like as the service begins.

"So now," she continued, "we're going to start the service over. And the choir is going to process in with us as they do for the Compline Service at St. Mark's Cathedral in Seattle, singing a Gregorian chant we got from the choir director at St. Barnabas on Bainbridge.

"We'll be robed in garments from St. Paul's," Gemma continued, "and we'll be using service leaflets – Joyce and Eleanor, could you begin distributing those please? – from Good Samaritan, one of our newest congregations, a startup that meets in a school cafeteria on the Sammamish Plateau. They use service leaflets because they don't have enough prayerbooks to go around, and because there are lots of people attending there who have never been to an Episcopal church before and haven't quite got the hang of juggling the prayerbook, the hymnal, and the service music the way you do.

"And one last hint: our service music today was written by an Episcopalian on Mercer Island. I'm bringing it to you as yet another way to share my past with you: the first Episcopal Church I ever attended, back when I was in college in New Hampshire, used this music. Every church has its favorites, of course. But for me music becomes irrevocably attached to experience, and to me this has always been 'real' church music. Just as," she added, " the music *you* use every Sunday makes church 'real' for you.

"Which," she went on, "is why I have no plans to change your music (in case you were worried). All these experiments today are just for today, to let you know a bit of what's out there and to help you understand what in means to be Episcopalian in other congregations.

"Anyway, before each bit of new service music, I will have the choir sing it through once so you have a chance to familiarize yourself with it. I'm told that this music was brought to Good Sam by one of their parishioners from All Saints Episcopal Church in Pasadena. That's one of the biggest Episcopal churches on the west coast; has anyone here ever worshipped there?"

Two or three parishioners put up their hands. "Oh, good," said Gemma. "Then you may remember the music and help us to sing it. Isn't it fun, what a small world this is?"

Seeing that Joyce and Eleanor had finished distributing the service leaflets so kindly donated by Good Sam, Gemma signaled the choir to begin, and they began processing in to the rich strains of Non Nobis Domine, Psalm 115.

Things went surprisingly smoothly, given that they were dealing with so many changes; the service leaflets simplified things considerably. And when Harry read the Psalm, Gemma was greatly reassured by "because He is at my right hand, I shall not fall," and then remembered what part of the Psalm had struck her – "indeed, we have a goodly heritage," which, when she thought about it, fit in much better with the rest of what she was undertaking today than the sermon she had preached at the previous service.

So, after hastily making a couple of notes on her Sunday bulletin with the pencil she always kept handy for last minute sermon thoughts, she offered up a quick prayer and stepped forward to read the Gospel, a rather unpleasant passage from Mark about the endtimes.

"Before I begin my sermon," said Gemma after a brief prayer, "I want to warn you about the Lord's Prayer. Many of you are aware that the Episcopal version of that prayer is different from that said by, say, the Presbyterians: we use the word "trespassers" and they use the word "debtors.""

"Some of you may also be aware that there are actually two versions of the Lord's Prayer in our prayerbook; the one we rarely use asks that we forgive sins instead of debts or trespasses.

"I'm sure you are all probably aware that as Episcopalians we are part of a larger group called the Anglican Communion. And I'm sure you suspect that across that communion, despite our common prayerbooks, there are even more differences in worship than we are encountering today.

"One of the most astonishing differences is in the Maori translation of the Lord's Prayer which is found in the New Zealand version of the Book of Common Prayer, and today we will be using that version. I want to ask you in advance to listen carefully as we pray that version; you'll find the text for it in your service leaflets. At the close of the service you'll have an opportunity to let us know if you learned anything about the familiar version of the Lord's Prayer from listening to the unfamiliar one.

"So today." Gemma continued, "we heard in the Psalm, 'Indeed, I have a goodly heritage.' And it struck me that that applies beautifully to what we are doing here this morning as we expose ourselves to the broader heritage of the Episcopal Church; to rituals appreciated by other congregations in our diocese and beyond. Many of us come to church because it provides a safe constant in our lives, a place where things stay the same, where things and people behave predictably.

"And for many of us, that familiarity is as much or more of a solace and consolation in times of trouble, pain, grief or confusion as is the presence of God. Sometimes even moreso, because church is something we can touch, feel, hear, smell. We love the familiar music, the scent of the altar candles, the taste of the wine – which reminds me, today we'll be using Port, courtesy of Epiphany Episcopal Church in Seattle.

"We're used to the familiar dry crackle of the wafers, too, but today we'll be using bread baked for us by the altar guild of our little church in Forks, Washington – way out on the farthest reaches of the Olympic Peninsula. And I hope you'll welcome their visiting parishioners," she added, beckoning an older couple in the back of the church to stand. "Meet Anita and Greg

Merlotti, who decided to bring us the bread from Forks and stay at the Inn for the weekend."

"The problem with doing it always the same way," Gemma continued after the Merlottis had reseated themselves, "is that even though it may provide comfort, that comfort can get in the way of actually hearing what God may be trying to tell us. The words of the service, the songs and the hymn become so familiar that you don't even hear them anymore.

"It's a little bit like a marriage -- and I am not the first person to use that analogy – where one partner takes the other for granted. Some of you, I'm sure, know what that feels like, when your mate just assumes you will always be the same, and ceases to pay attention to you. Sometimes you just want to shock them into awareness, just so they will listen to you for a change. Because we all like to be heard, to feel special, to be attended to, to feel that what we have to say is important. And sometimes when we don't get that for long periods of time it takes a big shock to wake us up and make us pay attention.

"Well, if we are made in God's image, it's my guess that God might want us to pay attention to him just as much as we long for attention. And we all know God is totally capable of shocking us if he wants us to listen up.

"So I'm asking each of you to pay attention today. Because at the end of today's service we'll be passing the offering plate. You may have noticed that there are post-it note pads tucked in where the visitor cards usually go on the backs of the pews. Instead of giving money, I want each of you to give your attention – to God. I want each of you to write, on at least one post-it note, at least one thing that you learned about God today while worshiping differently. And I want you to put that note to God in the offering plate when it comes around.

"Joyce and I will be summarizing those comments and distributing them with the next newsletter, and then we will have a little bonfire after church next Sunday in which we burn your comments as a burnt offering to God. The ashes from that fire will join the ashes from Palm Sunday that we've been storing in the back room, and will form part of the ashes for next spring's Ash Wednesday service.

"If you did bring money for the offering, and you want to give it anyway, I invite you to place it in the little white model van we have out in the Narthex. That toy van, as you'll see from the sign above it, is for the collection of money to re-institute that old island institution, the Snow Goose. Any offerings you put in the van today will go 100% toward refurbishing the Goose so St. Elwood's can again begin serving those of our community who find it difficult to get to the Mainland.

"And I've said these things to you," said Gemma, "in the name of the Father, who wants to hear from you and be heard; of the son sent to love you, and of the spirit who broods over creation like a mother over her children. Amen."

Gemma sat down, stunned. And hoped they actually did store ashes in the back room. And that St. Elwood's actually offered an Ash Wednesday service. Whatever she had anticipated, it wasn't that they would give up this Sunday's offering – not at a time when the church was hurting for money. But she had spoken as she had felt led to speak. Now she'd just have to wait and see what developed.

CHAPTER 22

Gemma could tell that some of her parishioners were a little put off by Eucharistic Prayer C, the one her former parish, Good Samaritan, Sammamish, used for their communion service. She loved the phrase "This fragile earth, our island home" and thought it a perfect match for a church in the San Juans, but when they got to "from the primal elements you brought forth the human race," she could see Marcia hissing into her husband's ear, trying to wake him up. When they came to the Lord's Prayer and Marcia encountered the line in the New Zealand version about "father and mother of us all," she hissed particularly loudly and stood up, forcing Orville to stand up as well.

Marcia looked angrily around at the other parishioners, but most of them had their noses buried in the service leaflet and were reciting the prayer, paying careful attention to the words. She harrumphed and said in a loud voice, "I've had about enough of this New Age folderol; come on, Orville," and then began to extricate herself from her pew.

Unfortunately the two people at the far end of the pew had elected to use the fold-down kneeler for the prayers, and there was a rather complicated scuffle as she attempted to press forward before they could get the kneeler all the way up. The kneeler dropped back down and apparently landed on Orville's toe, because he yelped and fell against Marcia, forcing her to explode awkwardly out of the pew. By this time all pretense of prayer had ceased, and members of the congregation stared as Marcia led the way out the side door with her husband limping uncomfortably behind her.

Gemma paused a beat, then took up the prayer where she had left off when the kneeler dropped, and the remainder of the Eucharist proceeded smoothly. After the post-communion prayer, Gemma came down the steps into the central aisle and invited everyone to take a moment to think about the day's service and then fill out a post-it note. When people appeared to be done writing, she had Eleanor and Joyce pass the collection plate.

When the two women came forward bearing the two plates full of notes, Gemma blessed the plates as usual, saying, "All things come of thee, O Lord, and of thine own have we given thee," and then invited the congregation to join her in the closing prayer.

After the prayer Agnes launched into Onward Christian Soldiers and Gemma, Harry and Darla processed out behind the choir.

"I'll go set aside those collection plates," said Harry. "I expect this'll be real interesting!"

"Thanks," said Gemma, and she positioned herself by the door to see what the responses to the morning's service would be.

The first few people to leave seemed to have enjoyed the variety of the morning's service, commenting cheerily about various wordings or music they liked. Several specifically mentioned their appreciation of the chant that had begun the service, though no one seemed quite willing to abandon Rock of Ages.

As Gemma was chatting with those folks, though, she saw a number of old-timers choosing to leave by the side door, and her heart sank. What if her experiment had failed? What if, instead of opening up a new world to her parishioners, she had permanently alienated them? She tried not to think about the implications of their departure, and returned her focus to the greetings at hand.

"That Marcia," said Doris, shaking her head. "I'm sure she expected everyone else to leave with her."

"… or at least the rest of the folks in her row," chimed in Shari.

"Yeah," said Darla, coming up with Joyce. "That was *so* awkward; you'd think they could have at least waited until everyone was standing so they didn't trip over the kneelers!"

"Now, Darla. I expect she'd just had about all she could handle. Bad enough Orville was snoring during the prayer of confession," said Joyce.

"Yup," chimed in Fiona, "That's probably the loudest I've ever heard him."

"Hmm," said Gemma. "Perhaps he has a low blood pressure problem."

"I'll just say this: if he does have low blood pressure," said Joyce, "Marcia is the perfect antidote!"

"Well," said Gemma, choking back a chuckle and hoping to change the subject, "thanks for helping out, you guys; have a great rest of weekend."

"You, too," they chimed, and Gemma turned to greet the next parishioners.

Later, in the sacristy, Gemma turned to Harry.

"Coffee?" she asked.

"Can't today," said Harry. "My daughter's coming in on the noon ferry with her boys; we're gonna spend the afternoon together before they head up to Victoria for a week's vacation."

"Sounds like fun," said Gemma, "– how old are her kids?"

"Seven, nine, and three," said Harry. "And the three-year-old's a handful, let me tell you. I have to go home and move a bunch of stuff into a locked closet before he gets there; he's a breaker."

"Wow, sounds serious," said Gemma.

"Nah," said Harry, "he just hasn't quite figured out how to contain his energy yet".

"Well, good luck with that – and you'd better run, if you're gonna do that and make the ferry."

"Yup," said Harry. "See you later."

"Take care," said Gemma.

"You, too," said Harry, and he closed the door behind him.

Gemma finished straightening up, took one last look at the altar to be sure everything was cleared and ready for the altar guild, then locked the sanctuary and headed into her office.

Closing the door behind her, she sank into the leather chair and kicked off her shoes, sighing deeply. Resting her head against the wing, she began the familiar process of winding down after a service, closing her eyes, breathing deeply, and allowing her mind to drift over the course of the morning. Who was it she had seen going out the side door? She was mentally casting back over that moment when the phone rang, startling her out of her reverie.

"St. Elwood's, this is Gemma Benson," answered Gemma.

"So, how did it go?" boomed the bishop's voice over the line.

"Oh, God, Sam – why didn't you warn me?"

"Warn you about what?" asked the bishop.

"About the problem with overseas mission?" Said Gemma. "I presume you knew about this? Is there a reason you neglected to inform me about this minor detail? I just preached a sermon about the importance of mission and then I learned we could lose the building over it."

"Ah, Gemma," said the bishop. "You know the rule. "Landmines everywhere; always check for landmines."

"Yes, Sam, I know the damn rule. But you could at least have warned me."

"Now, Gemma, I can't think of everything. And look at it this way – now you know, it'll be less of a problem."

"Yes, but what do I do about the problem I already caused?" asked Gemma.

"I'm sure you can just claim ignorance – you know, the George Bush defense? Fool me once, shame on you, fool me twice…"

"You can't get fooled again," chimed in Gemma. "Like that's any help. You had better hope that flies, because otherwise you're gonna see this charming building turned into a community theater."

"What's that?" asked the bishop. "I couldn't hear you, too many trucks going by."

"Where are you?" asked Gemma.

"On I-5, coming back from Chehalis," said the bishop. "Their second service is at 9:30, not 10, so we got out early and Margaret needed to be back for some shindig in Seattle."

"Ah," said Gemma. "Well, give her a hug for me. Anyway, it turns out that the senior warden not only dislikes women clergy but she also walked out during the New Zealand Lords prayer…"

"Dragging her snoring husband behind her?" asked the bishop.

"How did you know?" asked Gemma.

"It's my job to know everything, said the bishop. "But also – just about every priest I've ever put in there has complained about his snoring."

"Oh," said Gemma, "so it's not just me!"

"Nope."

"Anyway, not only is she opposed to just about everything I stand for, but she's also a direct descendant of Elwood Bartenstein, and she's the one the church reverts to if I screw up. Apparently she wants to turn it into a community theater if it won't provide her idea of a perfect service."

"Hmm, yes, I'd heard that," said the bishop. "Well, Gemma, I'm sure you'll do whatever it takes to bring them into the 21st century without losing the building. Gotta run, kiddo; we're getting off the highway and the traffic looks pretty bad. Good luck!" the bishop added, and he rang off just as Gemma was gearing up to do some serious shouting.

She was tempted to throw the receiver across the room, but instead she curled forward and set it down on her desk, then leaned back again in her chair. *So much for supporting the flock,* she thought. *Well, I won't think straight unless I get some food in my system, so I might as well head home. Maybe take a nap after lunch; I hear Einstein had all his best ideas after waking up from naps...*

CHAPTER 23

Gemma made her favorite lunch: pita pockets stuffed with melted jack cheese, tomatoes, sprouts, avocadoes and mint, then garnished with a long dash of soy sauce. She was just wiping her hands after the last messy bite when the phone rang.

"Hello?"

"Hi, Gemma, it's Joyce. I couldn't wait to see what people wrote on their post-it notes, so I've been looking through them. You won't believe – or maybe you would. Anyway, it's an experience. Shall I bring them over to your place? Do you just want to compile the notes yourself, or can we work on this together?"

"Wow, sounds like this stuff's got you excited! Let's definitely do it together – but be sure to take some time off Monday to compensate," she added.

"Oh, I don't think Monday would be a good time to take off," said Joyce. "I suspect our phone's gonna be ringing off the hook for a few days; you'll need me there to run interference for a while, is my guess."

"OK. Sounds like we should definitely do this. Wanna bring them over here? Bring Darla along, if you like; the landlords left some fun books and games around the house if she doesn't just want to do her homework. I don't suppose you want to give me the short form over the phone," she said hopefully.

"Trust me," said Joyce: "there isn't one. These are all over the map!"

"Just be careful not to lose any," said Gemma

"Will do," said Joyce. "We'll see you in about half an hour."

"Well," said Gemma to herself after hanging up the phone. "So much for my nap!"

She put some water in the teapot and put it on the stove to simmer, then tidied up her lunch dishes and did a quick cleanup pass through the living room. By the time Joyce and Darla had arrived, she had a lively fire going in the stove and some of the landlords' more entertaining games were set out on the dining room table.

She was, of course, in the bathroom when they arrived. "I'll be right out," she called. "Make yourselves at home."

When Gemma emerged from the long hallway leading to her bathroom she heard the teakettle starting to whistle in the kitchen.

"Can I offer you some tea?" she asked. "Hot chocolate?"

"Sure," said Joyce. "Darla?"

"No thanks," said Darla. "Do you have any coke?"

"Nope, sorry," said Gemma.

"Never mind," said Darla. "Can I work on your bed?"

"Go right ahead," said Gemma; "spread out if you need to. The little dresser in the corner folds down into a desk," she added.

"No thanks," said Darla; "I'm used to working on a bed."

"That's what she said," grinned Joyce, and Gemma laughed.

"Mom!"

"Sorry dear, it just slipped out."

"Gross," said Darla, and she began emptying her backpack out onto Gemma's bed.

"Sorry," said Joyce.

"No problem," said Gemma. "Does this mean you watch The Office?"

"Oh, God, yes!" said Joyce; "I'm addicted."

"Me, too," said Gemma "– it's why I try never to schedule meetings on Thursdays... I'm SO glad it's choir practice and bridge night! Fewer phone calls to interrupt..."

"Fabulous," said Joyce: "I knew I liked you!"

"Feeling's mutual," said Gemma with a grin. "Now, let's see those post-its..."

Joyce started spreading the post-its out on the table, but there wasn't enough room for them all – clearly several people had written more than one. – and they decided to move to the living room floor. Joyce moved the chairs aside while Gemma poured the tea out into two cups and set them on the terracotta tiles by the fireplace.

"So where shall we begin?" Gemma asked.

"Well, I took the liberty of sorting them into groups," said Joyce. "And I marked all the really quotable ones with a red pen."

"I see," said Gemma.

"So these are the ones that talk about music," said Joyce, laying them out on the beige Berber carpet beside the fireplace. "And these are the ones that talk about the words of the service. There are a bunch about that New Zealand Prayer and Marcia's departure – I've put those over here. And this batch is the largest," said Joyce.

"What are they about," asked Gemma.

"Requests for change completely unrelated to today's service," said Joyce.

"What?" asked Gemma.

"Apparently there are lots of people who felt they weren't being heard," said Joyce.

"I see," said Gemma. "What sort of things are they asking for?"

"Hmm," said Joyce. "Well, several people objected to the cheap toilet paper in the restroom…"

"Oh, God," said Gemma.

"Yes, well, this is an older congregation…"

"I guess," said Gemma. "Were any of the suggestions service-related?"

"Oh, yes," said Joyce, "all these other categories are related to the service.. And we haven't even gotten to the complaints yet."

"Oh," said Gemma. "And are there many of those?"

"Depends," said Joyce.

"On what?"

"On whether you mean the complaints about the service or the complaints about Marcia leaving…"

"And the relative volume of those would be…"

"Two to one," grinned Joyce. "There were twice as many complaints about Marcia as there were about the service."

"Well, that's good, I guess."

"Oh, I haven't even gotten to the best part yet."

"What's that?"

"Hey, mom," yelled Darla from the other room, "did you tell her about the van yet?"

"What about the van?" asked Gemma.

"Well, I was saving the best part for last. Harry asked me to lock up the toy van we're using to collect funds for the Snow Goose?"

"And?" prompted Gemma.

"There was a thousand dollar bill in there," said Joyce.

"A thousand dollar bill? You're kidding! Was it real?"

"I called Harry to come and check it out, and he's not sure," said Joyce. "He's gonna take it to the bank on Monday to get it approved."

"Whoa," said Gemma. "I thought they stopped circulating those back in the 70's. Do we know who put it in there?"

"Not a clue," said Joyce. "I didn't know they even *made* thousand dollar bills."

"Wow," said Gemma. "Too bad we set the offering for the van today; that would have definitely taken care of that septic pumping bill Harry's so worried about."

"I think it's a good thing," said Joyce. "That Paulie can wait for his money; we need to get the Snow Goose going again."

"True," said Gemma. "Well, this will be a fabulous kickoff, that's for sure – if the money is real." She sat back on her heels. "Okay, so let's talk about these post-its."

Two hours later they had sorted and re-sorted the notes into categories and subcategories, and Gemma had written up the ones she wanted to use to inform the next few services.

"Thanks so much for your help, Joyce," she said, handing her the tan carcoat she'd left on the hook by the door. "Darla, thanks for coming over; did you get some of your work done?"

"Oh, yes," said Darla. "I got my math homework all done, and the science report; now all I have to do is read another 30 pages of *Cry the Beloved Country* and study for the history test on Tuesday."

"Well, good luck with that," said Gemma.

Darla shrugged into her jacket and reached for her backpack. "Do those things still weigh a ton?" asked Gemma.

"Mom says so," shrugged Darla. "Guess I'm just used to it."

"C'mon, Darla; we gotta get home and feed Jake," said Joyce.

"See you guys," said Gemma, and she shut the door behind them.

Maybe now I can get that nap, thought Gemma, as she stretched and arched her back. She was getting too old to be kneeling on a hard floor for such a long time.

Hungry, she wandered into the kitchen, but the refrigerator was pretty empty, and she didn't want to make another pita sandwich, so she decided to scramble some eggs instead.

Curled in front of the freshly stoked fire, Gemma chewed half-heartedly on her eggs. How should she present the post-it results? she wondered. How to talk about the observations voiced in their notes without alienating anyone? It would be a challenge, she was sure.... A challenge she'd be more up to after a good night's sleep.

Giving herself permission to crash, Gemma slipped into her fleece jammies and crawled under the flannel comforter. Tomorrow she would find out about the thousand dollars and begin crafting a report for the congregation.

CHAPTER 24

On Monday morning Gemma was awakened by the phone at 9:15.

"So those thousand dollar bills were taken out of circulation in '69," said Harry.

"And a fine morning to you, as well," said Gemma sleepily. Venice jumped up onto the bed and began kneading the pillow next to her face in a rather determined fashion

"Oh, I'm sorry; did I wake you?" asked Harry. There was no obvious apology in his voice.

"It *is* my day off," said Gemma pointedly.

"Who sleeps after 8 these days, anyway?" asked Harry. "There's so much to do, so much to see. If you sleep in you might miss something."

"Right," said Gemma with a yawn. "So what does that mean, anyway?"

"After 1969," Harry went on, "any time a thousand dollar bill showed up at a bank it got sent back to the feds to be destroyed."

"Why?" asked Gemma.

"Something to do with organized crime laundering money, I think," he replied. "But the important thing is, what that means is that the bills became sort of like guns, you know: if you outlaw guns, only outlaws will have guns? When they outlawed the bills, the only people left who had them were collectors and outlaws."

"So what, you're telling me the bill is no good? – Venice, get off!," she said, pushing the cat off the bed. "I'm *up* already!"

"Oh, it's good all right. The problem is, it's probably stolen goods."

Gemma went into the kitchen and put the phone on speaker so she could spoon coffee into her French press.

"Okay," said Gemma, "so…"

"So this one's probably illegal," said Harry.

"But isn't that a good thing, that someone's ill-gotten gain is now going for good?" she asked, setting food out for Venice

"Maybe, but the cops want to know where we got it."

"From the collection van!"

"But they want to know who put it there."

"But we don't know who put it there, or even when they put it there," said Gemma, feeding a log into the woodstove.

"Right. So now the police want a complete list of everyone who was in church on Sunday."

"What? We can't give them that," said Gemma. "That's a violation of privacy!"

"Well, that's how I'm trying to paint it," said Harry. "I'm trying to make certain they understand that we have a constitutional right to protect the identity of our parishioners."

"Where are you?" asked Gemma, a bit belatedly, as she began realizing that there were some odd noises coming through in the background of Harry's call.

"Well, actually, that's why I was calling," said Harry. "Um, I'm at the station; the police brought me in, and they need you to vouch for me, that I'm not the one who put in the thousand dollar bill."

"But even if you were," said Gemma, taking the teapot off the stove as it began to whistle and pouring water into the French press. "Ah," she said, as the coffee aroma began to fill the kitchen.

"What's that?" asked Harry.

"Oh, nothing, I'm just breathing in the coffee aroma," said Gemma.

"Well could you put it in a cup and come down here to the station?" asked Harry. "Because I need you to vouch for me, and I also need to get my daughter and the boys back down to the ferry."

"Which ferry?" asked Gemma.

"The 10:45," replied Harry.

"And are they just walking on?" asked Gemma.

"Yes, but…"

"Tell you what; I'll go pick them up and bring them to the station, then when you get released you can drive them from downtown."

"You're assuming I'll be released," said Harry.

"Well, why wouldn't you be?" asked Gemma.

"Because they've traced this bill," said Harry.

"And?"

"Turns out it's connected to some drug cache from this commune they raided on the island back in '94," said Harry. "The cops had a tip, but when they made the raid there wasn't as much coke as they had expected. At about the same time there was an accident on the island that killed this Seattle guy?"

"Wait," said Gemma, as the coffee and Harry's words began to penetrate her early morning haze. "Are you saying this money was connected with a murder?"

"No, like I said, it was just an accident. But apparently when they ID'd him there was a warrant out for his arrest. He'd been videotaped stealing from this collector in the U district who specialized in large bills. So then the Chief suspected there was a connection between this thief guy and the commune but he was never able to prove anything. Now this money looks to be back in circulation, they think they may be able to re-open the theft case and implicate some of the members of the commune."

"So does this commune still even exist?" asked Gemma.

"Not any more," Harry replied, "but several of our parishioners were... um... formerly associated? I guess that's common, to get religion while you're in rehab? And, well, most of them were here Sunday."

"Shit," said Gemma. "Do you know any lawyers?"

"We can talk about that later," said Harry cautiously. "Right now I just need you to get me *out* of here!"

"Okay, Harry, will do. Shall I pick up the kids or not?" asked Gemma.

"Don't bother," said Harry. "If you'll just get yourself down here I should be able to pick them up and get them to the ferry in plenty of time."

"Got it," said Gemma.

After hanging up, she threw on some clothes, ran a comb through her hair, grabbed her peacoat and headed for the car, cell phone in hand. She dialed the church.

"St.-Aidan's-by-the-Sea, this is Joyce."

"Hey there," said Gemma. "Have you talked to Harry yet this morning?"

"No, why?"

"We've got a problem; could you meet me at the police station in 10 minutes?"

"Sure thing," said Joyce.

"… and bring that toy van we're using for the Snow Goose Collection," said Gemma.

"Will do," said Joyce, and she hung up.

Gemma backed around the tight circle in front of the cabin, almost hitting the corner post of the carport, and sped out to the road. *Think*, she thought to herself; *where could that money have come from?*

By the time she got to the station, Gemma had a plan. She met Joyce outside and beckoned her over. "Okay," she said, "I don't have time to explain; just come in with me and follow my lead."

"Okay…" Joyce frowned.

Together they strode into the station. Gemma approached the young officer at the front desk. "Hi," she said, holding out her hand. "I'm the Reverend Gemma Benson, the new interim vicar at St. Elwood's. I gather you're holding Harry Borden?"

"Yes ma'am, er, father Benson, er…"

"You can just call me Gemma," she said, shaking his hand vigorously. "And what's your name?"

"Pete," replied the officer. "Pete Lawler."

"Okay, Pete, can you tell me where I can go to get this straightened out?"

"Just down the hall there," said the officer, "second door on the right."

Gemma and Joyce proceeded down the hall, and Gemma poked her head into the second doorway. "Harry?" she asked.

"He's right here," said another officer, a tall broad-shouldered man with graying hair and an air of authority. "You must be Pastor Benson?"

"That's me," said Gemma, "and this is our office administrator, Joyce Finley."

"Yes," the man said, staring fixedly at Joyce. "We've met." A slow flush rose in Joyce's cheeks, and she looked down at the floor.

"So what seems to be the problem, officer?" asked Gemma.

"Harry here came into the bank this morning with a stolen bill," said the man. "I'm Chief Henderson, by the way."

"Nice to meet you," said Gemma. "So. Is the problem that you think Harry stole the money? Surely by now he has explained that we found it in our Snow Goose collection van."

"Well, that's what he says. But if that's true, why won't he tell me who was in church on Sunday?" asked Henderson.

"But what difference would that make?" asked Gemma.

"Well it would certainly narrow down our list of suspects," said the Chief.

"I don't think so," said Gemma, looking at Joyce. "You see, it was Joyce who put that collection van out in the narthex. And it's been out there since Friday evening."

Joyce looked up at Gemma, blinked, and then turned to Chief Henderson.

"That's right," she said. "I – I put it out myself before I left work Friday evening. We get tourists in sometimes over the weekends, so I thought it wouldn't hurt to leave it out there, maybe collect some more money."

"Was it empty when you set it out Friday evening?" asked the Chief.

"Yes, it was. So you see, it makes no difference who came to church on Sunday, anybody could have put that money in there. So could you please let Harry go?"

"Yes," said Gemma. "Could you please release him now? Hold me, if you need to, but Harry needs to get his daughter and her boys to the ferry."

"Allright," said the Chief. "You can all go. But this isn't over with. There's a story behind this bill, and I mean to get to the bottom of it."

CHAPTER 25

"Um, Gemma?" said Joyce when they were out of earshot of the station.

"Yes," said Gemma, waving goodbye to Harry as he drove off to pick up the kids.

"How do you feel about perjury?"

"What do you mean?"

"That collection van didn't go out until Sunday morning. I didn't even buy it 'til Saturday," said Joyce.

"What?" said Gemma, stopping dead in her tracks. "I thought that was one of Darla's old toys. Didn't you say you remembered her having one, and you were just going to paint it and put it out there?"

"I did," said Joyce. "But it turns out it was broken and shabby. I didn't think it would send the right message. So we stopped by the Exchange on Saturday and picked up a red one; I painted it white that afternoon, let it dry overnight, and put it out on Sunday morning before the 8 am service."

"Oh, God," said Gemma, "why didn't you say something? What if someone at the Exchange remembers you buying the truck?"

The Dump Exchange was a Brandon's Rock institution. Occupying several acres of land off the main highway between the recycle center and the Grange, the Exchange was a place where islanders could bring items they didn't want anymore and either leave them for others to pick through or exchange them for other used items they might need. The main barn was divided into rooms which housed electronics, hardware, mattresses and kitchen goods, and there were covered walkways where people could leave everything from roller skates and bicycles to washing machines, toilets, and screened doors.

Open Tuesdays (for islanders) and Saturdays (for tourists), the Exchange was a lively spot and business was usually pretty brisk on Saturday afternoons. But it was unlikely that the attendant would forget that Joyce had come for the truck, as they'd had a pretty long conversation about why she wanted it and where to get what kind of paint to turn the van from red to white.

"I think we're gonna have to go back to the station and come clean," said Gemma.

"But won't they jail us for perjury?"

"I don't know. But maybe if we explain... hey, maybe the bill was already there when you picked it up at the Exchange?"

"But how would they know that?" asked Joyce.

"Wouldn't there be white paint stains on it?" asked Gemma.

"Oh, true," said Joyce. "There would be, and then that would let *all* of us off the hook. Let's do it."

"Maybe since we're coming back so quickly they won't have written up the interview yet and we won't be held culpable?"

"We can only hope," replied Joyce. They looked at each other, shrugged, and headed back up the steps into the police station.

"Hello, again," said Gemma to the young officer by the door. "We need to see Chief Henderson."

"It's important," added Joyce, "we have new evidence in a case."

"I'll see if he's available," said the officer, and he picked up a phone. "Have a seat over there, and we'll call you," he said, pointing to a long green bench by the door. One end was occupied by what appeared to be a drunk, sleeping it off, and next to him two parents were arguing while their teenaged son tried to be invisible.

Gemma and Joyce sat as far from the others as they could and stared guiltily at the floor.

"OK, ladies, what's this new evidence," said Chief Henderson, looming over them with a clipboard in his hand. "And make it quick, I have work to do here."

"Um, can we talk to you privately?" asked Gemma.

"Ok, come on back," the Chief beckoned, "but this better be good."

They returned to the room they had been in before, and Gemma shut the door after them.

"Um, we, um… we kinda need to explain something," said Gemma.

"Yes," said the Chief, his arms crossed over his chest.

"It's really my fault," said Joyce…

"No, Joyce, I'm responsible," said Gemma.

"Ladies, can we get to the meat here? I haven't got all day."

"Well," said Gemma, "it turns out Joyce actually didn't put the toy van out in the vestibule on Friday when she left work. Umm… she kind of hadn't gotten it yet."

"I was supposed to use an old one of Darla's," said Joyce, "but it was all banged up, so I thought I'd check the Exchange on Saturday to see if I could find a better one. But really, Gemma didn't know, and I didn't want her to know I hadn't done it, and we both really really didn't want to tell you who was at the service on Sunday."

"But we had another idea," said Gemma.

"Now let me get this straight," said the Chief. "The van didn't go in the vestibule Friday afternoon? It didn't actually show up until Sunday after all? and you *lied* to me?" He glared angrily at Joyce, who hung her head and shrank back against the wall.

"You need to understand," said Gemma. "Yes, she picked it up at the Exchange on Saturday. But it was a red van, so she spent Saturday afternoon painting it white. We thought it might be possible that the thousand dollar bill was already in there when she picked it up. And if it was, there'd be white paint splatters on it, and then you'd know for sure it wasn't anybody at the church."

"You know this is a punishable offense," said the Chief. "I could nail you two for this."

"I know," they both chimed meekly.

"But since you appear to have reported the problem as soon as you realized it I'll let you off the hook this time. Understand, I'm not saying there's paint on this bill, or even that if there is it means the bill was in the van when you got it from the Exchange. But I'll look into it. In the meantime, get in the habit of telling the truth; you can get into a lot of trouble if you don't."

"Thank you," said Gemma. "We appreciate your understanding and leniency."

"Thanks Jim," said Joyce. "I'm sorry. I never meant…"

"Enough," said the Chief. "Now you two get out of here and let me get some damn work done."

As they left the building Gemma noticed the boy had scooted way over to the other end of the bench and the argument between his parents appeared to have escalated considerably. Gemma waved goodbye to the officer on duty and closed the door behind her.

CHAPTER 26

Once out on the street, Gemma looked at Joyce, who was wiping her eyes. "That was awkward! But I think we did the right thing."

"Yes...," gulped Joyce.

"Come on. Let's get over to the church and see if we can't scare up some coffee. Something tells me there's more going on between you and the Chief than meets the eye."

"It's old history," said Joyce. "It doesn't really matter."

"Looks like it matters to him," said Gemma. "And my guess is it matters to you, too. I sense a story here. Alex says I'm like a hound when I get the scent of a good story, so you better just spill and get it over with."

"Okay," sniffed Joyce. "No reason why you shouldn't know; everyone else on the island does."

Joyce unlocked the side door of the church, and Gemma went into the kitchen to roust up some coffee. Going through the cupboards, she found an old tin of hard cookies and another with a dusting of international coffee, so she set both tins out on the table, fired up the teapot, set out two cups, and wandered into Joyce's office humming the "celebrate the moments of your life" theme from the old international coffee commercials.

"What are you..." Joyce asked, following Gemma out to the kitchen. "Oh, I see. I'd forgotten that tune; this is so sweet! You're crazy. It's not that good a story."

"Doesn't matter; I'm all ears," said Gemma. "You want to sit at the table, or shall we go into my office?"

"Office," said Joyce. "It's more private. You never know who's gonna wander through here, plus I'm expecting Darla will stop by after school."

"Got it," said Gemma. "Office it is," and she ushered Joyce in, set the cookies and her coffee cup down beside the winged chair, and shut the door.

"OK," said Gemma. "Spill it!"

"Well," said Joyce, "as you probably realize, I was married to Darla's father."

"I tend not to make assumptions about those things," said Gemma, "but, yeah, okay."

"So Jim was Ted's best friend; Ted was on the force at the time."

"Really," said Gemma.

"Yeah. So when Darla was about 3, Ted and I had been having some problems, and there was this waitress named Bitsy who worked at the Vinoy, you know, the resort down at the south end of the island? So Ted started, you know "working late," claiming he was out on a case and Jim had to cover for him."

"Uh-huh," said Gemma.

"Well, the long and the short of it is that one of those nights when Ted was "working late," Darla had been pretty peaky all day, and by about 1 am she was running a really high fever. We only had the one car, and Ted had it, so I was trying to track him down so we could get Darla over to the clinic; I didn't want to bug the EMT squad. So I called the station and Jim said Ted was out on a case, but he would come get me.

"So he did, and we were at the clinic with Darla (who turned out to have meningitis) when the emergency vehicles came screaming in. There had been an accident down at the Breakers Curve, drunk driver of course, and they were bringing in the victims. The drunk, who had been driving a pickup, was DOA. But the other driver and his passenger were in critical condition.

"Turns out that driver was Ted; he died about two hours later without regaining consciousness. His passenger, who hung on for a couple of days before she kicked the bucket, was Bitsy; they'd been out joyriding in our CRX, which was totaled in the wreck, of course.

"Jim had known what was going on, and hadn't wanted to tell me cuz he was protecting Ted. But I lost a husband and a car, and I almost lost Darla as well."

"Phew. That's a lot of stuff to hit at once: sounds pretty rough," said Gemma.

"Yeah, it was pretty bad. Jim's marriage wasn't doing too well at the time, either, and he sort of made a few moves in my direction to "cheer me up" but I wasn't interested in being anybody's other woman, so I just shut down. She later left him anyway; turns out she'd been having it on with a guy on one of the other islands. But by then the whole thing was just too awkward."

"Hmm." said Gemma.

"Don't get any ideas," said Joyce. "This is all just history."

"But neither you nor Jim ever remarried," said Gemma.

"Yeah, well, that doesn't mean we had the hots for each other," said Joyce.

"Oooh, a little sensitive, are we?"

"A lotta people were assuming we would hook up after the accident," said Joyce. "But it just didn't happen, okay? Let it go, Gemma. Darla and I have a good life here; I date occasionally… I don't need a man fulltime in my life, and neither does she."

"Got it," said Gemma. "And I'm sorry about the mess with your husband."

"Old news," said Joyce as she stood to leave. "It was a long time ago. I'll get back to work now; thanks for listening. You need anything?"

"No thanks," said Gemma. "And thanks for telling me."

"No problem," said Joyce. "It's not like it's news or anything."

"Right," said Gemma. "Just news to me."

"Just so you know?" said Joyce.

"Yeah?"

"Darla will be coming by after school to do her homework."

"No problem," said Gemma. "See ya."

"Yup," said Joyce, and she shut Gemma's office door behind her.

Gemma threw the empty coffee tin in the trash can beside her desk, refilled her cup with hot water, dropped in a teabag and curled back up in the wing chair. The tension between the Chief and Joyce had been pretty thick; her guess was the Chief had a thing for Joyce but hadn't been able to get past the barriers Joyce put up after Ted died. Or, she thought, maybe he just felt too guilty about his role in the mess to feel he had a right to ask anything of Joyce.

Whatever it was, it might be worth talking to the Chief again. Maybe she could turn up some new evidence to take him. Gemma began trying to think through what new evidence might look like, but soon gave up. Better get to work preparing the post-it report; she had procrastinated long enough.

CHAPTER 27

Sometime around mid-afternoon Gemma remembered that Monday was supposed to be her day off. She decided to abandon the post-it project for a bit, and headed to the grocery store to stock up for the week ahead.

While in the checkout line, Gemma caught sight of Jasper sitting at one of the deli tables by the front door. "Hey, Jasper," she said, pushing her cart towards the door.

"Hey," said Jasper.

"You got any dinner plans tonight?" asked Gemma.

"Nah, Mom's on the mainland again," said Jasper.

"I was thinking takeout pizza sounded good. Whaddya think of pepperoni? Wanna eat out with me?"

"Maybe," said Jasper.

"Tell you what," said Gemma, reaching into her purse. "We could use some ice cream for dessert, but I don't want to go back through the lines again. Here's some money; just wait until about quarter to 6, then pick out whatever ice cream flavor you want – I eat anything – and bring it out front; I'll pick up you and the ice cream at 6 and we'll go back to my place and eat."

Gemma held out a $5 bill, and Jasper took it from her. "You sure?" he asked.

"Yup," said Gemma "Just don't let me down: ice cream's not on my diet, but if you buy it it doesn't count!"

"Yeah, right," said Jasper, rolling his eyes.

"Hey," said Gemma. "It's your call – 6:00, be there or be square. Deal?"

"Deal," said Jasper.

But at 6 Gemma pulled into the grocery store lot and there was no Jasper. She parked and went into the store to look, even asked after him, but no one had seen him and he was nowhere to be found. She waited near the door until after 6:30, then drove over to Unca Joe's, picked up the pizza, and swung back by the store. Jasper was still missing, so on a hunch she called Joyce.

"Have you seen Jasper?" Gemma asked.

"No," said Joyce, "why do you ask?"

"He was supposed to meet me for dinner," said Gemma, "and he didn't show. I thought maybe he came by the church."

"Hmm," said Joyce. "Maybe you should check over at his house?"

Joyce gave her directions to the trailer park where Jasper lived with his mom, and Gemma headed out toward that part of the island, nibbling on her pizza.

The trailer park was dark when Gemma pulled in. There had obviously been street lights at one point, but only one was working, and the light it cast was pretty feeble. Most of the rest had broken lenses, and the trailers all had a bit of a seedy look, what she could see of them. Following Joyce's directions, she turned down the third lane and looked for the green trailer on the left with the striped and broken awning.

Pulling in to the space beside the awning, Gemma opened the car door and stepped out into a graceless yard of dried mud and gravel. There was a rickety carport at right angles to the trailer, but no car, just an old washing machine, a couple of bikes with flat tires and a motley collection of boards and old toys.

Gemma walked up the makeshift wooden steps to knock on the trailer door, but there was no answer. She knocked again, and then pushed the button on the handle to see if the door was unlocked. It swung slowly in with a loud creaking squeal, and she stepped into the darkened trailer.

"Hello?" Gemma called. "Hello-o. Jasper?"

The trailer was silent, and there was a faint smell of garbage emanating from the kitchen. Gemma turned to leave when she heard a moan from somewhere inside.

"Hello?" she called again. "Is someone there?"

The sound came again, a little louder. It seemed to be coming from down the hall. Gemma groped around for a lightswitch but could find none, so she went back out to her car for a flashlight.

Back inside, flashlight in hand, Gemma shone it around the room. The place was a mess, as if a tornado had blown through. Surely they didn't actually live like this, she thought, and then automatically stifled that reaction. Best to follow the sound, see if someone might be hurt.

She shone the light around the living room again and picked out a light switch on the far wall, so she stepped across the debris and flipped it on. A lightbulb in the ceiling overhead came on, and feeling a little safer, she went down the hall, following the direction of the sound.

It seemed to be coming from the last door on the right, but she peered in each of the rooms she passed, just in case. The rooms were surprisingly tidy; she found herself wondering why the living room was such a mess in comparison. And in the last room she found the source of the moans.

"Jasper!" exclaimed Gemma. The boy was lying on the floor in the middle of a pool of blood littered with shards of broken glass; the remains of a lamp lay next to him.

"Jasper, are you okay? What happened?" asked Gemma. The only response was a moan, so she checked his pulse, then pulled out her phone and dialed 911. "It's an emergency, this boy's been hurt," said Gemma, and she gave the directions for Jasper's trailer. "Please hurry, there's a lot of blood and I can't tell where it's coming from and he isn't talking," she said.

"Jasper, honey, it'll be okay; they're sending someone right over," said Gemma, going back to the boy. "Can you sit up?" Gemma felt his back and neck, and then realized the back of his head was sticky. Somehow he must have fallen against the lamp, knocked it over, and knocked himself out? It seemed unlikely, Gemma thought. Could it have been a break-in? But who would break into Jasper's trailer? It was tidy enough, except for the kitchen and the living room, but there didn't appear to be anything worth stealing.

Gemma put a towel over a pillow and placed it under Jasper's head, then went into the kitchen to look for a broom and dustpan. She had cleaned up most of the broken glass when she heard the distant squeal of the sirens; by the time the flashing lights pulled into the driveway she had scooped all the glass into the dustpan and dropped it in a paper bag. A pre-emptive knock sounded at the door of the trailer, and she opened it to find herself face to face with Chief Henderson and Pete Lawler.

"Thank God you're here," Gemma said. "I hope you brought some medics with you; it's Jasper and he seems to be pretty badly hurt; I found a wound on the back of his head, and he still hasn't responded to me other than moaning."

"They're right behind Pete," said the Chief, and he stepped aside to motion them forward.

"Last room on the right," said Gemma. "He's still on the floor where I found him."

"So tell me, Pastor Benson, what brings you to Jasper's trailer?" asked the Chief.

"We were supposed to meet for dinner at 6," said Gemma. "I was planning to pick him up at the store and take him back to my place for pizza and ice cream but he never showed, so I thought I'd check here. The door was open, the lights were off, and I heard him moaning in the back room so I came in to check it out."

"I see," said the Chief. "And what did you find?"

"Well," said Gemma, "the living room is obviously a mess, but the other rooms are surprisingly tidy, almost as if somebody trashed this room but didn't get to the others.

"I found Jasper in the back, lying on his back in a pool of blood and broken glass; it looked like the glass came from a broken lamp that was lying nearby. Could he have interrupted a robbery in progress or something? Maybe the robbers hit him on the head with the lamp? The back of his head was all sticky when I checked it."

"Did he say anything?" asked the Chief.

"No, so far all he's done is moan."

"And what happened to all the broken glass?"

"I cleaned it up," said Emma. "It's all in that bag over there."

The Chief threw up his hands. "Don't you people watch TV? Don't you know better than to mess with a crime scene? I thought you Episcopalians were big into murder mysteries; you know, Dorothy Sayers and all that."

"Pete, grab that bag and take it down to the station; see if you can get any prints off the glass," he said, turning to his deputy. "And see if you can't track down Drew; we need to get him out here to keep an eye on the place, see if he can figure out where this guy went."

"Right, Chief," replied the deputy.

The medics came out with Jasper on a stretcher. "Right now we need to get this kid to the clinic, see if we can replace some of that blood he lost and get him to talk."

"That sounds so cruel, like he's the bad guy," said Gemma.

"For all we know he is," said the Chief. "Don't make assumptions."

"Right," said Gemma. "A nine-year-old boy trashes his own living room and knocks himself out on purpose so his mom won't know he was the culprit? I don't think so."

"Just don't make assumptions," said the Chief. "One step at a time, we'll get there."

"And Jasper could be dead," said Gemma. "We have to figure this out – I want to know who did this to him, and why."

"So do I," said the Chief. "But first we need to find his mother."

"I think Joyce knows how to reach her," said Gemma, eyeing the Chief. "I'll give her a call – unless you'd rather?" she asked.

"Nope, you do that, I'll see he gets to the clinic. Why don't I meet you there in…" he looked at his watch. "Shall we say 30 minutes? 7:45? Hopefully Drew will show up soon to keep an eye on this place."

"Okay," said Gemma. "I'll see if Joyce can help locate Jasper's mom and we'll meet you at the clinic by 7:45."

CHAPTER 28

The Clinic at Brandon's Rock was a low-slung red brick building located about a mile out of town on the north shore drive. Gemma and Joyce pulled into the almost-empty parking lot shortly after 7:45 and slid into the space next to the Chief's police car.

"You're late," growled the Chief, unlocking the front door for them. "Did you track down the mom?"

"How's Jasper?" asked Gemma.

"Stable, still not talking; you find the mom?" repeated the Chief.

"I called Suzanne's cell but she's not picking up," said Joyce.

"Probably out tying one on at the Triple," said the Chief.

"Or she could be on the evening ferry coming home from massage school," said Joyce pointedly.

"Oh, come on," said the Chief. "Massage school, really? Like that woman was ever capable of completing anything she started."

"That's not fair, Jim," said Joyce. "You know her family story; she has a lot of strikes against her. Give her some credit for trying."

"Excuse me," said Gemma. "I'm sure this is all very edifying but the critical question is Jasper. Can we see him?"

"I think if you let them know you're a priest they'll let you in," said the Chief.

"Great," said Gemma, looking around, "where do I go?"

"Here, just a second," said the Chief, and he reached down behind the reception desk and pushed a buzzer. Moments later a young woman in bright green scrubs covered with purple turtles appeared, wiping her hands on a small towel. "Can I help you?" she asked.

"Sundance, this is Gemma Benson; she's the new priest at St. Elwood's and she wants to see the boy. Gemma, this is Sundance; she's Doc Warburton's PA. She'll take you in back to see the kid."

"Hi," said Gemma, holding out her hand. "I'm the one who found Jasper; I was looking for him because he stood me up for our dinner date. How's he doing?"

"Well, he's lost a lot of blood, but thankfully it seems to be only a flesh wound; he'll have a pretty good sized bump in the morning, but that should be the extent of it. Once we've got his system replenished he should be good to go. Were you able to track Suzanne down?"

"No," said Gemma as they walked into a small brightly colored room where Jasper lay on a blue-sheeted hospital bed, looking very small and pale. "Joyce left messages at her house and on her cell."

"I hear she's been hanging with Bryce Wilcox, the dive guy," said Sundance. "You might try calling his place."

"Hmm," said Gemma. "Joyce did mention she hadn't seen Suzanne in a while; she may not know that. Could you go tell her? I'll be all right here; I promise I won't touch a thing."

"OK," said Sundance. "Just be sure if he wakes up to keep him in bed; he's pretty weak."

"Will do," said Gemma. Sundance left the room to find Joyce and Gemma pulled a chair up next to the bed. Taking Jasper's hand in her own, she silently breathed a prayer of thanks that his injuries weren't more serious, then followed it with a prayer for children and parents everywhere.

When Sundance returned, Gemma was still sitting at his bedside, holding his hand.

"Any change?" asked the PA.

"Nope, he's pretty quiet," said Gemma.

"So how'd you come to find him?" asked Sundance, and Gemma explained about the plan for pizza and ice cream and about the state of the house.

"That's odd," said Sundance. "Suzanne's really a meticulous housekeeper; I've never seen anything out of place in her living room before. So it had to be like robbers or something, but who would want to steal anything from there? I mean, it's just a trailer, and everyone knows Suzanne's barely able to make her rent."

"I don't know," said Gemma. "It's a mystery, for sure. We're hoping Jasper will be able to clarify things a bit when he wakes up."

"We've reached the mother," said the Chief, walking into the room with Joyce. "Her cell was out so she was using Bryce's; she's due in on the 10:20 ferry."

"Good," said Gemma. "I'll stay with him 'til she gets here; I'd hate for him to wake up and not have a familiar face at his side."

"Right," said the Chief. His pager buzzed, and picking it up he headed for the hallway. Gemma could hear him murmuring into the phone, and then he was back in the doorway. "I gotta run, there's a domestic out by the Exchange," said the Chief. "Joyce, can I give you a ride home?"

"No thanks," said Joyce stiffly. "I'll stay here with Gemma."

"You need me to check on Darla?" asked the Chief.

"No, she's at the Teen Center, I'll be getting her later," said Joyce.

"Well, then; guess I'll see you around," said the Chief, and he left.

"Still carrying that old grudge, eh, Joyce?" asked Sundance.

"Drop it, ok?" said Joyce.

"Right," said the other woman. "Well, I'll leave you two with Jasper. I'll go out front and watch for Suzanne; holler if there's any change."

"Thanks for staying, Joyce," said Gemma, still holding Jasper's hand. She smoothed back the hair on his forehead, absently checking for fever. "He looks so young, doesn't he?"

"They're all babies when they're sleeping," said Joyce. "Sometimes I peek in on Darla at night, and I can't believe she's almost a teenager. When she's asleep, she just… I look at her and I can still see the two-year-old in the crib."

"He just looks so vulnerable," said Gemma. "Why would anyone attack a little kid?"

"You know what I wonder," said Joyce.

"No, what?"

"I wonder if the guy who hit him wasn't still in the house when you got there."

"What do you mean?" asked Gemma.

"Well, it stands to reason – obviously they didn't find what they were looking for in the living room. But they missed all the other rooms, and then for some reason they were down at the end of the hall. I think they must have chased him down there, and then hit him. But once he was down, wouldn't they tackle the other rooms? I bet you came in just after the guy finished searching the living room, and he was hiding, like, behind a door or something."

Gemma shivered, and mentally went back into the trailer, looking for clues. Had she heard anything? She mentally retraced her steps: let's see, she found Jasper, then went to the kitchen to call 911… and then she remembered; there had been a noise. She had assumed it was Jasper, waking up. But maybe it was the intruder; was there a back door to the trailer?

"Oh, my God, you're probably right." Gemma looked at Joyce, wide-eyed with fear. "What if he was lurking down the hall and snuck outside while I was dealing with Jasper. What if he was just waiting for all of us to leave? What if he's gone back in? You should call the Chief!"

Joyce dialed the number on her cell and handed the phone to Gemma. "You tell him."

Gemma explained what was worrying her, and the Chief stopped her in mid-sentence. "Already on it, he said. I called in another deputy, Drew Bailey, he just didn't report in until after the medics were gone. I'm pretty sure whoever it was got away."

"Oh," said Gemma.

"How's the kid?"

"Still sleeping," said Gemma, "but he's starting to get a bit restless. We'll keep you informed."

"See that you do," said the Chief, and he hung up.

"No dice," said Gemma to Joyce. "He called in Drew Bailey, but by the time Drew showed up whoever it was was gone."

"Hmm," said Joyce.

"What?" said Gemma.

"I just never trusted that Drew."

"How come?"

"I dunno," said Joyce. "Just a feeling. He was part of the team handling that big drug bust back in '94, back when Ted was still alive. Something funny went down with that deal; they didn't take in nearly as much as the informants said they would find. But of course, that part of it never made the papers."

"I don't know," she added. "He's just always kinda given me the creeps. You know, like that Norman Mailer guy says – some cops aren't really so different from criminals. Just cuz they're on the right side of the law doesn't mean they're good people, you know?"

"I guess," said Gemma. "I don't have a lot of experience with either."

"Cops and criminals?" asked Joyce. "Or cops and good people?" she smiled.

"Hmm. Think I'll take the First on that," grinned Gemma.

"NO!" shouted Jasper suddenly, and he began struggling desperately with the covers.

"Get Sundance," said Gemma urgently, and she placed her hands on Jasper's shoulders, staring into his face and willing him to wake. "Jasper, it's okay, I'm here," she said, keeping her voice deliberately calm. "Jasper, wake up, look at me. It's me, Gemma. It's okay, you're safe now."

CHAPTER 29

Joyce ran back with Sundance in tow, and while Joyce soothed Jasper and Sundance checked his vital signs Gemma called the Chief on her cell.

"He's awake," she said tersely.

"Be right there," came the Chief's response.

Gemma hung up and returned to Jasper's bedside. Sundance had him sitting up against a pillow, but he was obviously very disoriented, though he seemed to calm somewhat when Gemma took his hand.

"It's okay, Jasper," she said. "Can you tell me what happened?"

"I was in my room playing video games and I heard a noise. I thought it was mom, coming home, so I called out to her. But this big guy in a mask came in and started shaking me, going "where's the money, where's the damn money" and when I said I didn't know what he was talking about he hit me."

"Do you think you'd know him if you saw him again?"

"I don't know, he was really big and he had this sort of growly voice. But I did manage to bite his wrist before he hit me," said Jasper.

"Really," said Gemma. "That was very brave of you."

"Well I didn't want him to find the money," said Jasper.

"What money?" asked the Chief, striding into the room.

Jasper's eyes widened when he saw the Chief, and he clamped his mouth shut.

Gemma sat down beside Jasper on the bed. "What money, sweetheart?"

"I wanted it for the Snow Goose, and for Mama," said Jasper.

"If you found money, you can certainly get a reward, son," said the Chief. "They might even let you keep some. But it's not your money; it probably belongs to someone else, and they might want it back."

"It's my money," said Jasper stubbornly, and he folded his arms across his chest.

"Son, I know you and your mom have had some tough times," said the Chief, sitting on the other side of the bed from Gemma and resting his hand over Jasper's on the sheet. "And believe me, I can guarantee that if you tell me about the money you'll get to keep some and give some to the Snow Goose.

"But if there's a lot of money, in big bills like the one you left in the Snow Goose collection van – that was you, wasn't it?" Jasper nodded, his eyes big with tears. "If there's a lot of money it probably means some bad guys stole it and hid it wherever it is you found it. If we don't get it back to its rightful owners those guys are gonna keep trying to steal it back from you. This time they only hurt you a little bit and scared you. But next time they might come after your mom, and you don't want that, do you?"

"No," sniffed Jasper.

"Then you need to tell us about the money, son," said the Chief.

"I didn't do nothing wrong, sir," said Jasper.

"I'm sure you didn't, son," said the Chief. "Why don't you tell us about it."

"So, after Gemma introduced me to Dr. Lindquist," said Jasper, "and his dog?"

"Yes," said the Chief.

"Well, I been going over there after school to walk Gunnar," said Jasper. "The Professor comes along, but he lets me hold the leash?"

"Yes," said the Chief.

"Well on Saturday the professor wasn't feeling too good," said Jasper, "so he let me walk Gunnar alone. And there was this squirrel, see, and Gunnar kinda jumped away from me and I let go of the leash? An' he ran off after the squirrel and chased it up into that old barn where the Professor keeps the Snow Goose?"

"Yes."

"Well the squirrel ran up into the rafters," said Jasper, "and Gunnar was barking a lot, and running and jumping all over the barn, trying to figure out how to get up to the squirrel, and I was trying to get the leash to take him back to the house. I almost had him, and then he got away again, and then the handle of the leash caught on something. And I thought, oh, good, I can catch him now. But then the squirrel jumped onto the floor and started to run out the door and Gunnar tried to run after him and the leash pulled whatever it was caught on and suddenly there was this big hole in the floor," said Jasper.

"You mean, like a trap door?" asked Gemma.

"Yeah, like in a computer game."

"So is that where the money was?" asked the Chief.

"Yeah," said Jasper. "There was this hole, and there was like a little stool in the hole, so I went down into it and it was kinda dark and I tripped over this like sheet thing."

"And?"

"Well it got tangled around my foot," said Jasper, "and when I went to pull it off it pulled away from the wall and there was this old suitcase."

"And that's where the money was?"

"Yes, in all these, like, clear envelopes."

"So what did you do with it?" asked Joyce.

"Well, I took one bill for the Snow Goose, and one for mom, and then I covered up the suitcase again and climbed out of the hole. I threw some extra straw down on it for good measure," said Jasper. "I couldn't figure out how to replace the trap door, so I just covered it up with a tarp," he added. "Nobody ever goes in there anyway, so I just figured I could go back when I needed more. Then I left the barn and called for Gunnar and he came right to me," said Jasper. "I took him back to the Professor and then went home."

"So the money's still there?" asked the Chief.

"I don't know," said Jasper. "I snuck into the church and put the money in the van, but when I went back to the barn to see if I could fix the trap door, somebody had already had done that and the tarp was gone. I couldn't figure out how to get it open again, so I left."

"Well, it sounds to me like we need to check out this barn," said the Chief. "What did you do with the money you took for your mom?"

"I'm not telling," said Jasper, folding his arms.

"I'm not trying to take it from you," said the Chief. "But every bill has a serial number on it. If we can look at the serial numbers, we might be able to figure out where the money came from. If you could give it to me, I could write a receipt for you, and then I'd be sure to give it back. If you like, you could tell Pastor Benson where you hid it, and she could bring it to me, where we could keep it safe for you."

Jasper looked at Gemma.

"I could do that, if you like," said Gemma. "Would you like the Chief to leave the room so it's a secret, just between us?" she asked. Jasper nodded.

"Okay, then," said the Chief. "Gemma, as a woman of the cloth I presume you're trustworthy. I'll see you down at the station – shall we say, in an hour? Joyce, how about if you go with her to wherever that bill is. You two would probably be safer together; we don't know what this guy knows or where he's gone," he added.

The Chief stood and shook Jasper's hand. "Thank you, son," he said. "You may be helping us solve a very important crime here; you've done some fine detective work."

"But it was all a accident," said Jasper.

"An accident you handled very well," said the Chief. "When we get all the money back we'll be sure to see you get the reward."

"Gee thanks," said Jasper. "That could really help my mom."

"No problem," said the Chief. "See you soon, ladies. I've asked Pete to come keep an eye on Jasper here; he'll be right out in the hall if you need him."

"So where is it, Jasper?" asked Gemma after the Chief had left the room.

"Well, you know that table the collection van was sitting on?"

"Yes."

"It has a drawer in it. I stuck the bill on the back side of the drawer with my chewing gum," said Jasper. "I figured God would look after it if I left it in a church."

"Wow," said Joyce. "That's pretty clever, Jasper!"

"At least the bad guys didn't find it," said Jasper.

"We hope,' said Gemma. "C'mon, Joyce; let's go check it out."

CHAPTER 30

After ensuring Pete was there to guard Jasper's door, Gemma and Joyce drove back to the church to look for the missing bill, which was indeed stuck to the back of the table drawer. They pulled it out and took it to the station, where the Chief quickly dialed up the database and checked the number.

"Well, that confirms it," said the Chief.

This bill is also from the von Gandringham heist."

"What's that?" asked Joyce.

"Alexei von Gandringham was a private collector in Seattle who specialized in those large denomination bills that the Nixon administration discontinued in 1969," said the Chief. "Some pretty savvy thieves managed to break into his home in the U District back in the spring of '94 and made off with all the bills he had in denominations of a thousand and greater.

The video cameras in his vault ID'd one of the robbers, but he turned up dead here on Brandon's Rock about a month later, and they were never able to track down either the other two guys or the money. I'm a little concerned that the stash was found in Doc Lindquist's barn, given his connection to the University, but I can't imagine he's connected with the theft in any way."

"There were a lot of hippie types who emigrated to Brandon's Rock in the late 80's and early 90's," added the Chief. "Most of them were just back-to-the-landers, and pretty much kept to the woods. There was a group of conspiracy theorists, kind of a cult; they built a couple of arsenals that are still on the island – we still have to train any new EMTs about those. And then there was that commune. Coulda been the folks that pulled the von Gandringham heist holed up with one of those groups: there was a big drug bust at the commune around that time, so there may be some connection there."

"What I don't get is how the professor is involved. But I'm guessing the dead guy mighta been visiting the professor, or housesitting for him or something. I'll interview him in the morning, see if he was connected to the guy they ID'd. No one came forward at the time of the accident, but he might have been using another name.

"In the meantime," said the Chief, "you ladies might as well go on home. It's getting pretty late."

"But what about the suitcase full of money?" asked Gemma.

"And the guy who hit Jasper," said Joyce.

"Yeah, there must be somebody still here on the island connected with the money," said Gemma.

"Well, they aren't going anywhere tonight," said the Chief. "The last boat off the island left about ten minutes ago, so I think we're safe for the night."

"They could already be gone," said Gemma.

"I don't think so," said the Chief. "Given what we know about when the guy hit Jasper, he couldn't have done that and made it down to the ferry in time to get off the island; the lines were pretty long today because of the long weekend."

"But the guy with the money coulda left," said Joyce.

"True," said the Chief. "But I'm thinking he wouldn't have known to look for it until the news came out about the G-spot, and that wasn't common knowledge even at the station until this afternoon."

"But what if whoever it is tries to take the red-eye off the island tomorrow morning?" said Gemma. "If you don't know who he is, how can you stop him?"

"Guess that's a risk we'll have to take," said the Chief.

"I don't like it," said Gemma.

"Not your problem," said the Chief. "You two ladies go on home; we'll deal with this."

Joyce and Gemma headed out to the parking lot. "I don't know," said Gemma. "You think we ought to hang out at the ferry dock tomorrow morning?"

"Well, I've been here since the '80's," said Joyce. "I could go down with you, maybe stop and chat with everyone I know who's been around that long."

"Seems like a stretch," said Gemma. "I think I'll just sleep in. I would like to go check on Jasper, though. When was his mom supposed to show up?"

"I think she was supposed to be on the 10:20 boat," said Joyce.

"Maybe I'll take him some ice cream, since I promised that earlier and he never got any. Then I can hang with him 'til his mom gets here."

"Sounds good," said Joyce. "I'm bushed; think I'll head on home – see you at the office tomorrow."

Gemma drove back to the church, dropped Joyce at her car, then headed for the soft-serve machine at the convenience store. As usual the store was crowded with teenagers, arguing and flirting; Darla was there, too, standing in the video section deep in conversation with a dark-haired boy in a nose ring and a Grateful Dead t-shirt. "I just dropped your mom off at the church," said Gemma. I think she's on her way to the Teen Center to pick you up."

"Oh, gosh," said Darla, looking at her watch. "I better run for it. She'll shoot me if she thinks I escaped."

Gemma paid for a vanilla cone and drove back to the clinic to give Jasper the cone before it melted.

Sundance met her at the door but didn't comment on the cone. "How's he doing?" asked Gemma.

"Seems fine," said Sundance, "but he's clearly got a whopper of a headache."

"Did his mom show up yet?" asked Gemma.

"Nope; ferry's been in a while, but she may have had to make another stop on the way into town."

"I think I'll sit with him 'til she gets here," said Gemma.

"Sounds good," said Sundance. "You got a friend, buddy," she said, nodding to Pete and opening the door into Jasper's room.

"I brought you a present," said Gemma, and she handed Jasper the ice cream.

"Thanks," said Jasper. "I was getting kinda hungry… did you find the money okay?"

"Yes." said Gemma, "We took it to the Chief and he put it in a bag with your name on it."

"Do you think it'll help solve the case?" asked Jasper.

"Sure thing; we already know where the money came from," said Gemma. "Apparently there was a big robbery down on the mainland in '94; both bills are from that collector who was robbed."

"Wow," said Jasper. "Docs that mean the money's been down in that hole for all these years?"

"Looks like it," said Gemma.

"How do you think it got there?" asked Jasper

"We're not sure," said Gemma. "The only guy they were able to ID at the time of the crime was killed here on Brandon's Rock shortly afterward. We think he must have hidden the money and then died in a car wreck before he could tell anyone where he hid it.

"There's gotta be at least two other guys involved in this though," she added, "the one who took the money after you found it (though I don't know why he suddenly knew it was there) and the guy who came after you looking for it. Did you tell anyone about it?" she asked.

"No," said Jasper, "cuz I was kinda hoping to leave it there and just use it when I needed it."

"But someone must have seen or heard you; was anyone around when you and Gunnar were romping around the barn after the squirrel?"

"Well," said Jasper. "There was a guy visiting the professor when I showed up to take Gunnar out."

"Who was he?" asked Gemma.

"I dunno," said Jasper. "I think he was like a former student or something."

"What did he look like?" asked Gemma.

"I don't know; I just heard his voice," said Jasper. "Mom!" he exclaimed, as a thin tired-looking woman with long wavy red hair came into the room. "You came back!"

"Gotta come back for my best boy," she said, giving him a hug. "Are you okay? That's a pretty big bandage on your head."

"Oh, mom, I thought it was you, and then it wasn't, and I was so scared and he was really big," said Jasper.

"I'm Gemma Benson, the new interim vicar at St. Elwood's," said Gemma, offering her hand to Jasper's mother. "And you must be Suzanne?"

"Yes, thank you, nice to meet you," said Suzanne absently, still focused on Jasper.

"I'll leave you two alone now. See you tomorrow, Jasper," said Gemma, but he didn't answer, and she closed the door gently behind her, leaving him in his mother's arms.

CHAPTER 31

The wind was driving the rain at a steep angle as Gemma drove home, and her car thermometer was reading 36 degrees, so she was especially careful going through the heavily wooded curves by the Exchange. The roads on Brandon's Rock were all two-lane, and tended to get pretty narrow at the outer edges of the island, so there wasn't a lot of room for error if things got slippery – though fortunately they rarely did, it being the temperate Pacific Northwest. Still, she was careful, having learned the hard way one night coming home from a meeting in Gig Harbor that the road can be colder than the car thermostat is reading.

Fortunately she had moved some wood into the house that morning before leaving, so it was dry and the stove lit quickly. She shrugged out of her wet jacket, put a pot of water on to boil, and climbed into her fleece jammies while Venice settled onto his cozy sheepskin pad by the stove. It had been a long night, and she was still wondering if perhaps she should be heading down to the ferry dock in the morning, though how she could stop the money from leaving the island was beyond her. What she really needed was to use her brain, sift through the evidence, and figure out who was responsible for hurting Jasper.

The teapot began to whistle, and Gemma poured water into a cup with an almond/orange teabag. Wrapping her hands around the cup to warm them, she curled into the chair by the fire and stared into the flames, hoping for inspiration. Finally she rose from her chair and sat at the dining room table with one of her lavender scratch pads and a felt tip pen. *Okay*, she thought, *here's what I know about the person (X) who hit Jasper:*

> *X was connected with the von Gandringham heist*
> *X was probably local, as he knew where to find Jasper*

X was large and male and owns a mask

X might still have been in the house when I called 911

X saw or was connected with someone who saw Jasper with one or both of the bills, but he didn't see where they were hidden.

X had to know the bills were the missing take from the heist.

X seems to have assumed that Jasper had all of the money, so he must not be the person who took the suitcase.

But if Jasper didn't take the suitcase, and neither did X, who DID?

Next Gemma pursued the question of Y, the person who took the suitcase.

Y may or may not have seen Jasper in the barn.

Y may or may not know that Jasper found the money

Y may or may not know that X knows about the money and is looking for it.

Here Gemma stopped: Y could be totally innocent! Y could be Professor Lindquist! What if he had gone in the barn for some reason, discovered the broken trap door, taken the suitcase and repaired the door? If so, she thought, he could be in danger – because if she could see that he might be Y, then X might figure it out as well.

Gemma tossed off her jammies and squeezed back into her slightly damp jeans. They were very cold, but she figured she could turn up the heat in the car. She slid back into her coat, threw another log on the fire for Venice, and then climbed into her car to drive to Professor Lindquist's place.

The temperature outside had dropped another 3 degrees to 33, and the wind had begun to pick up. The rain was lashing at the side of the car when she drove across the neck, and her headlights picked out the tips of the whitecaps in the Sound.

Gemma turned the car's heater way up and kept both hands tightly on the wheel, trying not to tense up. She safely negotiated the worst of the curves by the Exchange and continued on into town, past the convenience store and up the hill to the Professor's house. Heartened by the light she could see in the professor's upstairs window, she parked the car, grabbed a pocket flashlight, and headed up the drive to his house.

She had to knock several times on the door before it opened, and to her surprise it only opened a few inches.

"Yes?" said the professor.

"Professor, it's me, Gemma Benson, the priest. I stopped by the other day. I really need to talk to you – it's important."

"I'm sorry," he said, shaking his head oddly, "this is really not a good time."

"Please," said Gemma. "I know it's late; I promise I'll only take a couple of minutes of your time."

"I don't..." began the professor, and then the door flew open and Gemma saw a man in a police uniform holding a gun to the professor's head.

"Oh, no," said Gemma – "I'm sure he's innocent; you really don't have to hold him at gunpoint."

"Get inside lady," said the cop, and he grabbed Gemma's arm and yanked her into the house, keeping the gun on the professor and slamming the door behind her.

"But I'm innocent, too," said Gemma. "I don't understand."

"It's not us, it's him," the professor explained as the deputy gestured with the gun for the professor to move away from the door, dragging Gemma along beside him.

"What do you mean?" asked Gemma, and then she took a closer look at the gunman. He was a large man, with a thick beard, and she could see that where his sleeve had pulled back a bit there was a bandage on his wrist.

"Oh," said Gemma. "You're the one that hit Jasper. I can see where he bit your..."

"Shut up and move into the kitchen," interrupted the man. "I got a job to do here, and I need to be in the ferry line with the money by morning. So convenient, isn't it, that there's a HazMat workshop in Anacortes tomorrow. Chief's insisting I have to attend."

And of course, thought Gemma, the Chief would never think to check his own patrolman's car or prevent him from getting on the ferry. "Are you meeting friends over there to divvy up the money, or are you keeping it all for yourself?" asked Gemma.

"What do you think?" said the deputy. "I worked hard for this cash, an' I been waitin' over 13 years for the payoff. I'm not sharing *anything*: I finally got me a ticket off this rock, and I fully intend to use it, soon as the professor here tells me where he put the money."

"I don't know anything about any money," said the professor. "I keep telling you, Drew, I have no idea what you're talking about."

"That damn kid found the money me 'n' Harley took from your buddy in the U district back in 94. Damn Harley hid it and then got hisself killed before he told me where he put it."

"Harley?" asked the professor. "Harley Peterson? He was a thief?"

"Oh, yeah," said the gunman. "He sure had you fooled. He was a smart one, that Harley, kept a good cover for himself studying at the U. But it was all a sham. He'd been on the streets since he was 11; you can't take that out of a kid."

The professor backed up and leaned against the counter, crossing his arms behind his back. "So you and Harley were the men who stole my friend von Gandringham's collection of bills?"

"Yup. Harley figured to move the stash up here when he came up with you; that's why we timed the heist to coincide with your retirement dinner, cuz he knew you and the wife was coming up here right after. He just threw the suitcase in the back of your van and followed behind," said Bailey. "He musta planted the case in the barn that first night. The plan was to let things die down a bit, and then take it into Canada. But Harley got himself killed in that wreck on the curve, and never got around to telling me where he hid the money..

"But no matter now; you tell me where you put the damn suitcase, since it hadda be you that pulled it outta that hole in the barn. Tell me, and I'll let you and the little lady here off easy. Any trouble and I can kill you both and turn the house upside down; shouldn't take too long to find what I'm looking for – specially now that damn dog of yours is out of commission."

"Um, professor," said Gemma. "I think he means business. Why don't you just tell him where it is and he'll let us go."

"I'm telling you the same thing I told Drew, Gemma: I don't know about any money."

"Well then who does?" asked Bailey. "That bill didn't show up at the station until Monday, so nobody knew about it before then except the kid and that Harry, who thought it was like magic from God or something. And neither of them took the damn suitcase. So it's gotta be you."

"Look, professor," he said, cocking the trigger and turning the gun on Gemma. "I'm running low on time here. Tell me now or I'm taking out your little religious buddy here. I get that you don't have much to lose, but I'm betting she does. So speak up, old man," he said, jamming the pistol into Gemma's neck. "Speak up now, or she's history."

CHAPTER 32

Gemma had dropped Joyce off at the church, but before heading home, Joyce had gone back in to her office to run off some more copies of Gemma's post-it note report. The Xerox machine, which really needed to be replaced, had developed an overheating problem, and she could only print a few copies at a time before it would shut down.

So she ran another few copies, then headed back out into the rain to start her car, pick up Darla at the Teen Center, and head home. But the car didn't start. She called Gemma, but there was no answer. After trying two other friends with no luck, Joyce was stymied. Her instinct was to call the Chief, but after the vibes that had been flying back and forth between them these last few days she wasn't sure that was a good idea. She called Harry, but he wasn't answering either, so she gave up and called the station.

The Chief answered the phone himself. "Chief Henderson here," he said gruffly, in the voice she had once known so well.

"Jim, it's Joyce. I'm sorry to bother you, but I'm stuck at the church. My car won't start, and I need to pick up Darla and get her home."

"I'll be right there," said the Chief.

Ten minutes later Joyce saw the police car pull into the lot, and she stepped out to greet him.

"What's up, the battery dead?" asked the Chief, shouting a bit to be heard over the wind and rain

"No, I think it's the starter," said Joyce. "It's been pretty erratic lately, but I can usually get it running with a jump start."

"Pretty foul weather to undertake that," said the Chief. "Why don't I just drive you over to the teen center, pick up Darla, and take you both home. We can deal with your car in the morning."

"But how will I get to work?" asked Joyce.

"Tell you what," said the Chief. "I know you were itching to get down to the ferry dock tomorrow morning to catch the money thief. Why don't I pick you up early and we'll both head down to the dock, and then I can drop you off at the church and get your car up and running after the ferry leaves."

"I guess that would work," said Joyce.

"Good," said the Chief. "Now get in and we'll go pick up that girl of yours."

The Chief drove slowly up the main street, keeping his eyes open for anything out of the ordinary, but it was Joyce who spotted Gemma's Subaru at the bottom of the professor's driveway, just before the turn to the Teen Center.

"Isn't that Gemma's car?" said Joyce.

"Certainly isn't the professor's," said the Chief. "Kind of a lot of lights on at the house, for such a late hour; wonder what's going on?"

"With all that's been going on, I don't have a good feeling about this," said Joyce. "Do you think we oughta go up and check it out?"

"Let me check in and alert the medics, just in case," said the Chief, and he radioed Drew Bailey.

"That's odd," said the Chief. "There's no answer. He's supposed to be watching Suzanne's place; hope nothing blew up there. Damn. I need to keep Pete at the hospital to protect Jasper and Suzanne. Wish I had another backup. Guess we better swing by Suzanne's first, see if we can figure out what happened to Drew."

"Do we have to?" asked Joyce. "This is really starting to worry me. What if I check on Gemma while you go by the house?"

"Ah, she probably just couldn't wait to stop by and ask about the money," said the Chief. "Come on, we'll go check on Drew and then come back by if you like."

"Ok," said Joyce, "but hurry."

"Roger," said the Chief, and he sped around the corner and up the hill to Suzanne's. The deputy's car wasn't there, and the house appeared to be empty and untouched. "So where the hell is Bailey?" mused the Chief. "I know he's leaving in the morning for that HazMat workshop in Anacortes; he should be here, not out gallivanting around."

"Can we please go back to the professor's?" begged Joyce.

"Yeah, sure," said the Chief, "but I'd sure like to know where Bailey went." He backed the car out of the drive and headed out of the trailer park back toward town. "Do you want me to pick up Darla first?" he asked when they got to the intersection. "No," said Joyce. "She'll be safe at the center a bit longer. I really want to know what's going on with Gemma and the professor."

"Roger," said the Chief.

"Do you always talk like that?" asked Joyce.

"Like what?"

"You know – roger, ten-four... it sounds so... I don't know, old fashioned? Militaristic?"

"Never thought about it," said the Chief. "We spend so much time on our radios – there are only three of us, and the cell reception in many parts of the island is pretty bad, so the radios are just easier. Guess I get used to talking in shorthand. Might also be I'm... uncomfortable, nervous or something," he said, looking sideways at her as he paused at the stop sign.

"Oh..." said Joyce, and her mouth suddenly went dry. *Well, in for a penny, in for a pound*, she thought. "Um, Jim... About that night, you know, when Ted crashed. I've always wondered: did you know where he was?"

The Chief slowed the car a bit for the turn and took a deep breath. "The Seattle police had called earlier with the news that one of the guys identified with the U district heist had been seen at the Anacortes terminal, headed for Brandon's Rock. I sent Ted out on assignment to check the bars for unidentified strangers."

"Really?" said Joyce, her voice tinged with skepticism.

"Look, Joyce," said the Chief, pulling to a halt in the professor's driveway. "I'm not trying to cover up for him. I knew he'd been seeing Bitsy on the side, and I knew he was using this assignment as an excuse to connect with her. But you're so amazing, and she was such a... I don't know," he said, reaching into the glove compartment and pulling out his gun. "I guess I was hoping if he spent a little more time with her he'd see what a loser she was."

"Look, I better let Pete know where we are," he said, flipping on his pager. "Yo, Pete."

"Yup," came a rattly voice over the receiver.

"You seen Drew yet?"

"Nope. But he reported he was watching Suzanne's place for us. Nothing going on over there."

"Okay, listen. We're at the professor's place, investigating some suspicious activity. I'll leave this on and strapped to my belt so you can listen in. We may need a medic; not sure yet. If it sounds like you're needed, put a call in to the county sheriff over in Friday Harbor, leave Sundance with the kid and come up our way, you hear?"

"Ten-four, Chief," came the scratchy reply.

"You know, a funny thing," said the Chief as they headed up the dark drive toward the house. "The driver of that pickup did turn out to be the guy Ted was out looking for. So he found him. Just a little too late. The guy musta just planted the money in the professor's barn – wonder if he was on his way to meet someone?"

"We may never know," said Joyce.

"Maybe when we find the money we'll get the answer. For now you should probably be quiet 'til we see what's happening here," and the Chief knocked loudly on the professor's door. "Professor?" he shouted. "Gemma? Are you there?"

CHAPTER 33

"Not a word, you two," hissed Bailey as he prodded Gemma again with the gun. "Anybody know you're here?" he asked, pushing her in the direction of the kitchen.

"No," said Gemma, "but I left my car at the bottom of the driveway," she replied, and winced as he pushed her into the broom closet off of the kitchen. Bailey shut the door behind her and locked it. "You stay put in there," he said, "and keep quiet or your friend the professor is gonna have a new black hole to investigate."

"Ok, professor. Now lets answer that door, shall we? And don't try anything funny."

The professor shuffled awkwardly to the front door, pushed none too gently by the gun prodded in his back. He'd recognized the Chief's voice; what could he say or do to give the Chief a clue to what was sticking in his back? His brain raced to solve the problem as he shuffled slowly forward, propelled by the relentless prodding of Bailey's gun. And then, with no more time to think, he opened the door.

"Hey, professor," said the Chief. "I'm sorry to bother you so late, but I was driving Joyce home and she saw all your lights and spotted Gemma's car in your driveway. Is everything okay here? Is she about?

"Who, Joyce?" asked the professor, playing for time, and winced at the prod in his back.

"No, Gemma," said the Chief.

"Gemma Wesson?" asked the professor, "that priest?"

"Yeah, the priest," said the Chief, "but I think her name is…"

"No, she gunned it out of here a while ago," said the professor. "Um, do you mind, I gotta close the door or Gunnar will escape again."

"No problem," said the Chief, and Bailey kicked the door shut with his foot.

"Good job, old man; that oughtta hold him," said the deputy. "Now let's get your lady friend out of the closet and find that money."

The Chief gazed thoughtfully at the suddenly slammed door. "You know the professor's dog, Gunnar, right?" he asked Joyce.

"Yes, why?"

"Isn't he usually first to the door, and barking like a madman?"

"Yes, actually," said Joyce. "That's how Gemma first met the professor, because Gunnar got out and scared Jasper."

"So where's the dog now?" asked the Chief.

"I don't know, locked in the bedroom?"

"And why did he get Gemma's name wrong?" said the Chief, frowning, and then he smacked his head. "Shit! Shit! He said Wesson, and then he said she gunned it outta here. Someone's holding him – and maybe Gemma, too – at gunpoint, I'm sure of it."

"Pete, you get that?" he said into his pager.

"Yup," said Pete. "I'm on my way."

"Call the sheriff; get him to send a copter over," said the Chief. "And see if you can't track down Bailey; I'm thinking we may need reinforcements."

"Ten – four," said Pete.

"Joyce, I want you to go back to the car and wait for Pete," said the Chief.

"With Gemma in there risking her life?" asked Joyce. "I don't think so. How about if I knock on the door looking for Gemma, and you go around back and see if you can get into the house while I'm distracting them."

"I don't like it," said the Chief. "Too much risk of you getting caught in the crossfire – or being taken hostage."

"Tell you what," said Joyce. "What if I create some other kind of diversion?"

"Like what?" asked the Chief.

"Call Gemma's cell? She always keeps it with her," said Joyce.

"Nah," said the Chief, "he'll just tell her not to answer."

"We could set the barn on fire – but then we risk burning up the money, in case it's still in there somewhere."

"I think we need to just sit tight and wait for reinforcements," said the Chief.

"But what if he kills Gemma or the professor before they get here? We have to act *now*," said Joyce.

"All right," said the Chief. "You go to the front door and knock, but take it easy, okay? Any sign of trouble you run like heck."

"Got it," said Joyce.

"Okay," said the Chief. "I'll go around back and when I hear you knock I'll count to ten and head in."

Inside the house, the deputy returned with the professor to the kitchen, tied his prisoner to a chair using the remainder of the clothesline, and dragged the chair into the broom closet, next to Gemma. Pointing the gun at Gemma, he kicked at the professor's chair.

"Okay, old man; spill. What happened to the money?"

"I keep telling you, I don't know anything about any money," said the professor.

"What are you going to do to us?" asked Gemma, stalling for time.

"Nothing, if he tells me where to find the damn money," said Bailey. "I'll just leave you in here; someone's bound to find you eventually."

"But what about Gunnar?" she asked. "When he wakes up he's going to need to be fed and walked – it's bad enough you're picking on the professor, but what kind of cop deliberately hurts a dog?"

"The kind of cop that hangs out on the force 13 years hoping for a clue to the money he earned," said Bailey. "Did you think I was here out of the goodness of my heart?"

"But a dog?" wailed Gemma. "Surely you wouldn't deliberately hurt a dog."

"Enough discussion," said the deputy. "Tell me where the damn money is or I'll start shooting – and I'm starting with her ugly kneecaps," he added to the professor.

"Okay, okay," said the professor. "Leave her kneecaps alone. I'll get you the money. But you'll have to untie me; I can't tell you – I have to show you."

"Nice try, professor. But that's not gonna fly; I'll trust that someone with your education and command of the language can perfectly tell me where to find the damn money. Start talking, old man, or she's history."

At that moment a knock sounded at the front door.

"Jesus, now what," said Bailey. "Place is fuckin' Grand Central Station."

"Hold that thought, professor," he added, slamming the door to the broom closet, and he went into the living room and peered through the lace curtain.

"Damn, it's that secretary, Joyce. Probably saw your car in the damn driveway."

Gemma felt an irrational surge of hope. "Do you want me to talk to her?" she asked.

"Damn woman probably won't rest until you do," said Bailey. "All right. I'll untie you and you answer the door. Send her away, all nice like, and don't try anything, or I'll start with the professor's kneecaps," he added.

Bailey untied Gemma and walked her back to the door, holding her tightly from behind with the pistol stuck in her cheek. "Okay now," he said, as she approached the door, "Open it nice and easy."

"Yes?" said Gemma, opening the professor's door. "Oh, hi, Joyce. What are you doing here this hour of the night?"

"Hi, Gemma – I was on my way to get Darla, saw your car in the drive, thought maybe you were getting a jump on the Chief. Did you find out anything from the professor yet?"

"Um, no," said Gemma. "I was just heading home and thought I'd check up on him. I'll be leaving shortly. See you at work tomorrow?"

Bailey started to close the gap in the doorway, but Joyce stuck her foot in it.

"Okay," said Joyce. "But what do you want me to do about the post-it report?

Gemma winced as the deputy tapped her sharply on her shoulder blades with the gun and hissed "get rid of her."

"Um, be sure to get a copy to Jim," said Gemma. "I think there are things he needs to know," she said, improvising frantically in hopes that Joyce would get the message.

"No problem," said Joyce, giving her a quick two-thumbs-up. "He's already in the picture, but I'll be sure he gets the latest installment," she said, pointing to the side with one of her thumbs and attempting to show Gemma she understood.

"Great, Joyce," said Gemma, "I'll see you later."

"Will do," said Joyce, and she removed her foot from the door, which slammed a moment later.

Well, thought Joyce, *I've done my best to warn her. I hope the Chief managed to break into the house.*

CHAPTER 34

As she turned away from the door, Gemma heard a faint scraping noise in the kitchen. Joyce's frantic signals had convinced her the Chief was aware of the situation; was it possible he was already in the house? Perhaps a little distraction was in order, she thought. Keeping her head down, she turned suddenly and stumbled over Drew Bailey's foot. As if to steady herself, she continued twisting around and grabbed with both hands for the arm that held the gun.

As luck would have it, there was a coffee table behind him, and Bailey tripped and started to fall backwards. Unable to stop her momentum, Gemma landed on top of him. The gun went off, then spun out of Bailey's hand. Chief Henderson came rushing in from the kitchen to find Gemma sitting astride his deputy, who had been knocked out in the fall. The Chief looked questioningly at Gemma.

"He's the one who knocked out Jasper," said Gemma. "That's why he was so slow to get to the house."

The gun had slid across the floor into the Chief's path; the Chief picked it up and pointed it at the man who lay under Gemma. "What do you mean, slow to get to the house? Who is this character, anyway?" asked the Chief, and he reached down to turn the gunman's face toward him.

"What the fuck? What's Drew doing here, and what does he have to do with this mess?"

Keeping the gun trained on his deputy, the Chief gave Gemma a hand and she stood up. "Are you okay?"

"Nothing a little chiropractic can't fix," said Gemma, stretching her neck from side to side and twisting to ease the strain in her back.

"You know, Joyce should be here for this," said Gemma.

"Right behind you," said Joyce.

"But first we should get the professor out of the broom closet," said Gemma.

"I'm on it," said Joyce, heading into the kitchen while the Chief got on his pager to update Pete and the county sheriff.

Joyce and the professor rejoined them, bringing the rope that had been used to tie the professor, and the Chief tied off Bailey's hands and feet.

"So who's telling the story?" asked the Chief.

Gemma eyed the professor, then said, "I guess that's me," and began explaining what her list-making had led to. In turn, the Chief filled them all in on the background of the story, including Joyce's husband's role in the case.

"But where did the money go?" asked the professor.

"You mean you don't know?" Gemma exclaimed.

"I'd never heard of any money until tonight, when this 'policeman' came in, stunned my dog and started yelling about it," said the professor.

"Interesting," said the Chief, taking a long hard look at the professor. "I'm not quite sure I can believe that, but I think for now it will just remain a mystery."

An imperative knock sounded at the front door. "That's probably Pete," said the Chief. "We'll get Drew over to the airfield so the sheriff can deal with him; I'll follow up on this in the morning. For now I want you all to go to bed and sleep on it. Joyce, let's go get Darla; she's probably worried sick about you."

"I doubt it," said Joyce wryly.

"What do I do about Gunnar?" asked the professor.

"Let him sleep it off," said the Chief. "He should be back in form by morning. C'mon, Gemma, out!"

With a last quizzical look at the professor, Gemma followed the Chief and Joyce out the front door, thanked them for their assistance, and headed home.

The next morning Gemma was feeling pretty stiff from her fall. She took an extra long shower and some ibuprofen, then dressed and drove to the church. Joyce's car was in the lot, but the church was closed and locked, so Gemma let herself in and turned on the heat and lights. When, after half an hour, the Chief dropped Joyce off, Gemma raised an eyebrow questioningly at her assistant.

"Not what you're thinking," said Joyce. "My car wouldn't start last night, so he drove me and Darla home."

"And...," said Gemma.

"... and didn't stay," replied Joyce, rolling her eyes. "Somebody had to bring me back; my car's still out in the lot."

"I noticed," said Gemma, giving Joyce a long look.

"Look," said Joyce, "just back off, will you?"

"Right," said Gemma. "So, he got Drew airlifted over to Friday Harbor okay? I assume he suffered no permanent damage from my falling on him..."

"Yep, they took him in last night, and it sounds like the Sheriff managed to get a pretty damning confession out of him this morning."

"Terrific. Oh, and, by the way, thanks again for coming to my rescue last night."

"Looked to me like you did a pretty good job rescuing yourself," Joyce grinned.

"Yeah, well, I only decided to try something because you convinced me I had backup. So what do YOU think happened to the money?"

"I don't really know," said Joyce. "Do you suppose the professor is lying?"

"I'm not sure," said Gemma. "I don't think scientists are very good at lying; seems to me their whole deal is to uncover the truth. But then, you know what Einstein said," she added.

"What?"

"Whoever undertakes to set himself up as a judge of Truth and Knowledge is shipwrecked by the laughter of the gods."

"What the Hell is that supposed to mean?" asked Joyce.

"Well," said Gemma, "I suspect that right now it means we'd better get to work and stop trying to second-guess the gods. How are the post-it reports coming?"

"Good," said Joyce. "Only 20 more to copy and then we can distribute them to the congregation."

"Good," said Gemma. "Why don't I put together a cover letter, explaining about the video, the service, the report, the Christmas market, the Snow Goose and Eleanor. You put together this month's calendar; we'll run the whole thing by

Eleanor, and then see if we can't get it all mailed out before Sunday."

"Before Friday, you mean," said Joyce.

"Why Friday?" asked Gemma.

"Because if you drop the mailing in the island post office on Thursday, it'll all get delivered on the island Friday. If you drop it Friday it'll go to the main Edmonds branch and it won't make it back until Monday."

"Edmonds?"

"Yeah – any mail that comes into the island post office that either doesn't go to someone on the island or arrives after delivery on Friday morning has to go through the mail center in Edmonds."

"Okay, then," said Gemma. "I'll get typing. Maybe, in the interests of time, we should stop playing Kick the Can with our own Xerox machine and take it to the printers."

"Yeah, and with what money?"

"Let's take it out of the $1000," said Gemma. "We'll basically be piggybacking the mailing on the kickoff information for the Snow Goose Campaign, so I think we can justify that."

"You're assuming we'll get to keep that money," said Joyce.

"Hey, a little optimism never hurt anyone," replied Gemma. "So, what do you think – different colors for the different sections?"

"Whatever," said Joyce. "It all costs the same. Tell you what: I'll get started on the calendar while you work on the cover letter," and they both retreated to their computers and began typing.

CHAPTER 35

On Wednesday evening, after checking on Jasper at the clinic, Gemma had her promised dinner with Chandler Ferris. Though much of their time was spent rehashing her adventures with the professor, they also took time to talk about the church, and it was clear that Ferris had a lot of energy and talent to contribute to the St. Elwood's community. Gemma took the liberty of explaining the diocese's local priest program to him, and he seemed quite interested. Once the mailing was done she decided she would speak with the bishop about the possibility of staying on another year or two and working Chandler into a leadership role: it seemed like an ideal solution for a small community like Brandon's Rock.

By early afternoon on Thursday Gemma and Joyce had completed typing all the documents for the all-church mailing, and they were just waiting for the print shop to finish the last of the copies. Eleanor had read and approved the announcement of her temporary stint as Senior Warden, and had called in a few friends from the Senior Center for a stuffing party at the church, promising them a trip to The Pilings at her expense for lattes and cookies after the task was completed.

The stuffing party was just getting started when the Chief walked into the parish hall.

"Hey, Chief – did you come to help stuff envelopes?" grinned Eleanor wickedly.

"Nope," said the Chief. "I need to talk to Pastor Benson – is she around?"

"I think she and Joyce drove over to the print shop to pick up the last of the xeroxing," said Eleanor. "We're sticking the labels on to pass the time while we wait for them to return."

"Do you know where the keys to the rummage sale drop are kept?" asked the Chief.

"You mean the one out by the Exchange? What do you need those for? We just emptied it about a week ago."

"Just looking for some evidence," said the Chief. "Do you have access to those keys?"

"Well, sure," said Eleanor; "they're over in the office – come on, I'll show you," and she rose from the table and headed for the church office. Opening the bottom left cupboard door of the credenza across from Joyce's desk she pulled out one of several keys suspended from carefully labeled hooks on the inside of the cupboard door.

"This should do it," said Eleanor, handing him the key. "The lock is on the side furthest from the road, but I can't imagine you'll find whatever it is you're looking for."

"It's just a hunch," said the Chief. "I'll be checking at the Exchange as well," he added.

"Well, good luck finding whatever it is you're looking for," said Eleanor, "and thanks, by the way, for rescuing our priest the other night. She's a keeper; we'd hate to lose her."

"All in a day's work," replied the Chief as she walked him out of the office. When Eleanor returned to the Parish Hall, Gemma and Joyce were just coming in the back door, laden with boxes of printed forms for the mailing.

"Okay, ladies," said Joyce. "I think you all know Gemma Benson, our new priest?" There were nods and smiles of greeting on both sides. "She's gonna be shaking up St. Elwood's a bit – in a good way," she added, smiling at Gemma "– so this mailing is to let folks know what's happening."

"Now, I know some of you stuff from left to right and others right to left; I also know some of you stuff top to bottom and others bottom to top. So why don't you pair off with someone who does it the way you do, take a stack of each document, set it up in the order we need, and have at it."

The noise level in the room rose quickly as the women sorted themselves out around the tables. "Okay, ladies," said Joyce, when things settled a bit. "So here's how it goes: we want the white document on top; that's her cover letter, so put that at the beginning of your collating piles. Behind that we'll put the church newsletter; we've made that green for the holidays, so that comes second. The red flier is Marcia's piece about the

Christmas Market, and that goes third, and the set in yellow is the post-it note report."

"What's that?" asked one of the women.

"Well," said Gemma, "we had an experimental service last week, with hymns and anthems and readings and vestments from other churches around the Diocese, and we invited people to write down things they learned or liked or hated about the service on post-it notes after the service."

"The post-it notes went into the offering plate," added Joyce, "and any offering money was diverted to the Snow Goose."

"Oh, are they starting that up again?" asked one of the other women. "My Henry would be so grateful – he's been spending a fortune on his weekly trips to the oncologist in Anacortes."

"Oh, yes," added another. "I'm dying to get some more of that lovely brown rice we used to pick up from the Mount Vernon Co-op. I'll be happy to contribute to the Snow Goose Fund."

"Great," said Joyce. "Anyone else who wants to contribute, we'll have a little white collection van out in the Narthex after we finish today. Say -- does anyone know why the Chief was here?" she asked.

"He wanted the key to the rummage sale drop box out by the Exchange," said Eleanor. "Don't know what he'll find there; we emptied it just last week, and now that it's off-season it's pretty rare that people put anything in there."

"Hmmm," said Joyce, catching Gemma's eye. "I wonder what he's looking for?"

"Don't know," said Gemma. "But let's get stuffing; the sooner we get these envelopes filled and off to the post office, the sooner we can track down the Chief and find out what's going on."

Gemma and Joyce dropped the box of stuffed envelopes off at the post office just before 5 pm, and headed off to the Police station to see what was up with the Chief. He wasn't there, and Pete didn't expect him back, so the two women elected to stop by the clinic to see how Jasper was doing.

They found him sitting upright, playing with a battered looking GameBoy and sporting a brightly colored bandage around his head.

"My class from school came to visit," said Jasper excitedly, "and they all wrote on my bandage!"

"Didn't that hurt?" asked Gemma

"Nope, not a bit," said Jasper. "Well… maybe a little. But it was really cool, too!"

"I see," said Gemma. "Did the Chief stop by?"

"Yes he did," said Jasper, "and he showed me a picture of that deputy guy, Drew Bailey, in a mask. It was definitely him that hit me; I can't believe I was hit by a policeman!"

"Well, he wasn't a very good policeman," said Gemma," that's for sure. Most policemen are there to protect us, not to hurt us. Is your mom around?"

"The ferry should have landed by now," said Jasper. "She's sposed to be here any minute now."

Gemma sat and chatted with Jasper a bit while they waited for Suzanne. After a bit the door opened and Jasper turned excitedly to greet his mom, but it was only Sundance coming by to check his vital signs.

"How's he doing?" asked Gemma.

"Not too bad," said Sundance. "But he'll still need to be watched closely for a couple of days. That was a pretty serious concussion."

"I can do that," said Gemma "– if his mom needs to go to the mainland or something. She can always leave him with me."

"Good," said Sundance. "I'll get started on his release papers then."

Shortly after Sundance left, Suzanne knocked on the door and walked in to the room, her thin hands wrapped around a Styrofoam coffee cup for warmth. She greeted Gemma and sat down in the chair at the foot of Jasper's bed.

"So, how you doin', kid?" she asked, drumming her fingers on the chair arm. Where'd ya get the GameBoy?"

"I'm doin' great, mom!" said Jasper. "My teacher brought me this GameBoy from the school lost and found? And Sundance says they're gonna let me out this afternoon!" Suzanne looked at Gemma with panic in her eyes.

"I'll be happy to watch him if you have to go back to the mainland, Suzanne," said Gemma.

"Oh, would you?" asked Suzanne, lighting up. "I, uh, can't miss any more school or they won't let me graduate, and I really need this degree if I'm going to set up a massage shop here on the island." She stood and began moving restlessly around the room.

"It's no problem," said Gemma. "I'm happy to take him on."

"Great," said Suzanne, looking at her watch nervously. "That means I can probably make tonight's class after all. Jasper, honey, I gotta go catch the ferry. You be good, okay?"

"Sure, mom," said Jasper. "Will you be home tonight?"

Suzanne turned away from the door and came over to Jasper's bedside. "I don't think so baby, if that's okay with Pastor Benson. In order to make the last ferry I have to miss the last half hour of class, and I'd rather not. I'll come back tomorrow morning and check on you, okay sweetie?" she said, ruffling his hair.

"Okay mom," said Jasper sadly as he watched her leave the room. Suzanne waved goodbye again from the doorway and headed down the hall.

"It's hard to have her leave so often, isn't it Jasper," said Gemma softly.

"Yeah," said Jasper.

"Well, you're more than welcome to stay with me, tonight or any other night," said Gemma. "It gets kinda lonely out there at the Neck, you know; Venice and I are always glad for company."

Sundance came back in the room with papers to sign: with Suzanne gone Gemma needed to fill them out and accept responsibility. "What time can I come back for him?" she asked.

"Anytime after 7," said Sundance. "My shift will be off then, but I'll get his things packed up and let the night nurse know you're coming."

"Thanks," said Gemma, and she stood to leave. "See you later, Jasper – maybe we can have some of that ice cream we missed before I tuck you in tonight."

"Cool," said Jasper as she gave him one last wave from the doorway. "Tell Joyce I said hi, okay?"

"Will do," said Gemma, and she left the clinic.

Chapter 36

On her way home, Gemma stopped by the store and ran into the Chief in the parking lot. "Did you check the rummage drop box?" asked Gemma.

"Yup; nothing in it."

"Predictable, really," said Gemma, quoting from one of her favorite Monty Python sketches. "It was an act of purest optimism to have posed the question in the first place."

"Excuse me?" said the Chief.

"Never mind," said Gemma. "So I assume you were looking for the missing suitcase. Did you check the Exchange?"

"Yeah, there was a suitcase there that matched the description Jasper gave me. But no one could remember who dropped it off, or when – and, more importantly, there was no money in it."

"Did you take it anyway?" asked Gemma.

"Yeah," said the Chief, discouraged. "It's in the back of my car. I figure I'll run it by Jasper, and if it looks like it's the one, I'll have it checked for fingerprints."

"I'm picking him up at the clinic after dinner," said Gemma. "You want to meet me then?"

"Nah, I'm gonna head over now. That way, if it IS the one, I can get the fingerprints to the county before they close up for the night."

"Well, good luck with that," said Gemma.

"Thanks," said the Chief. "And thanks for all your help."

"No problem," said Gemma. "See you later," and she slid into her Subaru and headed home.

The Chief headed over to the clinic to show Jasper the suitcase.

"That's it, that's the one!" Jasper exclaimed. "See the sticker on the side? I remember it cuz it had that pyramid on it. Did you get the money?"

"No," said the Chief, "I'm afraid it's empty. I found it at the dump exchange this afternoon. No one there remembers when it came in or who brought it."

"Listen, Jasper," he said. "This is really important. Did you tell *anyone* about finding the money? Because the professor says he knows nothing about it, and clearly Bailey didn't find it."

"No, really, I didn't," said Jasper.

"Not even your mom?" asked the Chief.

"No one, I swear," said Jasper.

"Well, all right then, I guess we'll just have to hope the fingerprint test turns up something," said the Chief. "You take care, son, and let me know if you think of anyone who might have known about this."

"I will, sir," said Jasper.

The Chief left Jasper's room and headed out to the waiting room, where he encountered Gemma.

"Any luck?" she asked.

"Nope. He says he told no-one," said the Chief. "I guess we have to assume that someone was hidden in the barn somewhere, watching."

"But Gunnar would have seen them," said Gemma.

"You'd certainly think so," said the Chief. "Although, maybe he was distracted by that squirrel."

"Or maybe," said Gemma, "when he was trying to get into the loft, it wasn't just the squirrel; maybe there was someone else up there that he was after."

"Now there's a thought," said the Chief. "Maybe I'll go check out the loft, see if there are any signs of occupancy."

Heading out the front door of the clinic, the Chief turned to Gemma one last time. "Keep an eye on the boy, will you? It may be he knows something but just isn't aware of it. Even though Bailey is in custody, there's still someone out there who either has the money or knows where it's hidden. It's possible Jasper is in danger – there's always the chance some little clue will occur to him."

"Don't worry, Chief," said Gemma. "He'll be safe with me. And I'll see if I can't trigger his memory somehow. Have a good night," she added as she headed down the hall.

"You, too," said the Chief, and he shut the clinic door behind him.

"So, Jasper," said Gemma, walking into his room. "You ready for ice cream?"

"What flavor?" asked Jasper.

"Well, you get your choice: Vanilla, chocolate chip, or cookie dough," said Gemma... "with sprinkles, chocolate sauce, or whipped cream."

"Ooh!" cried Jasper. "Can I have cookie dough with all the trimmings?"

"One cookie dough sundae, coming right up," said Gemma.

The night nurse came into the room carrying a sheaf of papers and a brown grocery bag. "Ok, Mrs... Benson, is it? He's all ready to go, you just need to initial this last form. Here, young man, let's get you out of bed so you can get dressed."

The nurse handed her clipboard to Gemma and helped Jasper out of bed, giving him a minute to get his bearings. "Don't worry," she said, wrapping one arm gently around his shoulders. "You won't have to walk far; we've got a wheelchair for you. And you can stay in your jammies; just put on your shoes and coat so you'll be warm in the car," she said.

"I've put the rest of his things in this bag," she added, setting the bag by the door. "If he has any trouble sleeping you can give him one of these pills; I'll put the bottle in the bag with his clothes."

Gemma handed back the clipboard while Jasper tied his sneakers and settled into the wheelchair. "Okay," said the night nurse, "out you go," and she wheeled him down the corridor to the main entrance. "Why don't you go get your car and pull up by the door," she told Gemma. "I can carry him out to the car and get him situated. Do you think you can carry him into the house when you get home?"

"No problem," said Gemma. "Thanks for all your help."

"My pleasure," said the nurse. After Gemma pulled up, she carried Jasper out to the car and installed him in the front seat. Tightening his seat belt, she gave him a pat on the knee. "You take care now, big fella – and enjoy your ice cream!" Closing the car door, she waved goodbye to Gemma and headed back into the clinic, pushing Jasper's wheelchair before her.

"How are you feeling?" asked Gemma.

"Not so good," said Jasper. "My head hurts and I feel kinda dizzy."

"Sounds to me like you need ice cream and a good night's sleep," said Gemma. "Doctor's orders – coming right up!"

Later that evening, after feeding Venice and Jasper and tucking them both into the hide-a-bed in the living room, Gemma sat down to email Alex. She was pleased to find long emails from both her daughters, and began by answering those, promising to send Amy her winter boots and more money to Serena. Alex had dropped her a quick note describing a particularly difficult case at his clinic, and she, in turn, shared her concerns about Jasper, his absentee mom, and the missing money. She had already filled him in on the events of Monday evening.

I miss them all, she thought, as she turned off the computer and checked on Jasper one last time. She found him sprawled sideways across the hide-a-bed, with Venice curled, purring, against his neck. *It's a good thing things are so hectic here, I guess; I haven't had much time to think about family.* As she turned out the light she found herself wondering again: *what on earth happened to that money?*

CHAPTER 37

Gemma rose early the next morning and put the coffee on to boil, moving quietly lest she wake the sleeping Jasper. Venice, now dozing at the boy's feet, awakened and stretched, then padded into the kitchen, meowing insistently for breakfast. Gemma fed the cat, then called Joyce to say she would stay home and work on her sermon until Jasper's mother came for him; it seemed easier than waking him and taking him into town, and given the Chief's concerns she didn't want to leave him alone.

She had just sat down at her computer and begun typing when an imperious knock sounded at the front door. She went to the door as quickly as she could, hoping not to awaken Jasper. It was the Chief. She put a finger to her lips and stepped outside, nearly tripping over Venice as he darted out the door.

"What's up?" Gemma asked.

"It's the professor," said the Chief. "He's gone – and he's taken the Snow Goose with him."

"Oh, no," said Gemma. "Couldn't he just have gone to the mainland for supplies or something?"

"I don't think so," said the Chief. "I stopped by this morning to check out the loft in the barn, and I figured I'd just let him know I was around. There was no answer when I knocked at the door, and when I went in he was nowhere to be found. He seems to have taken off in a hurry, last night; his dinner was still on the table, half eaten. And when I went to the barn there was nothing to speak of in the loft and the Snow Goose was gone. I've got a call in to the ferry dock in Anacortes to see if he gets off the red-eye."

"But what if he doesn't show up on the boat?" asked Gemma. "Where could he go on the island?"

"I don't know," said the Chief. "And the problem is that with Drew gone I'm short-handed; I can't put out an all-points bulletin with only one man on the force. So I've called in to Friday Harbor for reinforcements, but of course it's at least another hour before they can get here."

"How can I help?" asked Gemma.

"I seem to remember something Joyce said once about a prayer chain," said the Chief.

"You want people to pray for the professor?" Gemma asked skeptically.

"No, it works like a calling tree, right? I was thinking you could use that to ask around, see if anyone's seen the Goose this morning."

"I think that could work... Shall I call Joyce or do you want to explain it to her?"

"If you could do it, that would be good," said the Chief. "She's not exactly speaking to me right now."

"I see," said Gemma, with an inquiring look.

"But here's the trick," said the Chief, ignoring her unspoken question. "If they saw the Goose, I need to know if the professor was driving, or if it was someone else."

"Who else would it be?" asked Gemma.

"I don't know," said the Chief. "But I'm beginning to think Drew had an accomplice."

"Really," said Gemma. "Do you know who that might be?"

"I have a hunch," said the Chief. "But that's all. What I really need are some answers."

"Okay," said Gemma. "I'll call Joyce and have her activate the phone tree. So what we want to know is: did anyone see the Goose, last night or this morning, and was the professor driving or was someone else. And if they get an answer, call the station?"

"Right," said the Chief.

"Okay," said Gemma. "I'll get right on it. Could you let me know if you hear anything?"

"Will do," said the Chief.

Gemma went back inside, took the cordless phone into her bedroom, and dialed the church.

"Joyce?"

"Yeah?"

"We have a phone tree, right?" said Gemma.

"Yup," said Joyce.

"Can you get that activated for me? Apparently the professor disappeared last night, taking the Snow Goose with him, and they don't think he got on the ferry this morning. Can you have people call around, see if anyone saw or heard him, or whoever was driving the Goose? Tell them to call the Chief if there's any news."

"Will do," said Joyce. "How's Jasper?"

"Still sleeping," said Gemma.

"And how's your sermon coming?"

"Oh, God," said Gemma. "Don't ask!

Gemma went back to her desk and turned on her computer, but she had lost whatever train of thought she'd had, and her mind kept returning to the puzzle of the professor and the money. Where was he, and was someone else involved?

After several false starts on the sermon, Gemma gave up, closed the laptop, and went into the kitchen for another cup of coffee. Hearing Jasper stirring in the living room, she crossed the room, perched on the edge of the hideabed and put her hand on Jasper's leg. He rolled over and sleepily opened his eyes.

"Hey, big guy," she said.

"Hey," said Jasper, blinking in the light from the sliding glass door.

"How'd you sleep?" she asked.

"Okay," said Jasper. "And my head feels better this morning."

"Good! Think you can handle a waffle?"

"With real maple syrup? And whipped cream?"

"I think that could be arranged," Gemma smiled. "Here, let me get the fire going in here; I didn't want to wake you before."

"Can I help?" asked Jasper.

"No," said Gemma. "Your job is to lie there and relax. I don't think I'm gonna want to give you waffles in bed, though; think you can make it to the table? Just take it slow and easy," she added, patting his leg. "We've got plenty of time."

CHAPTER 38

They had just sat down to their waffle breakfast when there was another peremptory knock at the door and Jasper's mother stormed in. "Jasper, where are you," she called. "Get your clothes on; we need to leave *now*."

"But Mom," said Jasper as his mom came into the kitchen. "We just started eating waffles. And there's real maple syrup, and whipped cream."

"I don't care if it's baked Alaska, you're out of here," said Suzanne.

"What seems to be the problem," asked Gemma, standing up to confront Jasper's mother. "I'm not sure he's ready to be out running around; he's still pretty woozy."

"We need to go," said Suzanne between gritted teeth. "Jasper, get your stuff and let's get out of here." Jasper left the table and began trying to tie his shoes

"At least let me carry him out to the car," said Gemma. "He can't walk very far on his own yet."

"You stay out of this," hissed Suzanne. "Jasper, now!" She grabbed the grocery bag with his clothes and dragged Jasper from the living room by his arm, one shoe still untied.

Gemma watched from the door as Suzanne half pushed/ half-pulled the boy down the driveway; there was no car in sight. "At least let me drive you to your car," she called, but Suzanne kept striding forward. When they disappeared around the curve, Gemma called the Chief, but there was no answer. On a hunch, she threw on her jacket and ran out to her car, backed around the circle, and headed out the driveway. Through the trees she saw a flash of white, and then, to her surprise, a large white van pulled out onto the road and sped off.

The van was going faster than Gemma dared drive on the narrow island roads, and by the time she got to the next intersection it was nowhere to be seen. She called the station again on her cell, but there was still no answer, so she called Joyce.

"Suzanne came and took Jasper – didn't even give him time to put on his shoes," Gemma said, "and I think she may have been driving the Snow Goose. I lost them on the way into town and I can't reach the Chief. If you see him could you tell him?"

"Did you try his pager?"

"I don't know the number."

"Ok, I'll call him. Where did you lose them?"

"At the corner of Cormorant Way and Brandon's Bay," said Gemma.

"Okay, I'll let the Chief know," said Joyce. "Stay in touch, and don't try anything risky – it sounds like Suzanne may be involved with the money. She could be dangerous," said Joyce.

"I'll be careful," said Gemma. "I'll let you know if I find anything."

Gemma turned right at the corner and drove slowly down to the water, scanning the heavily treed area for any flash of white, but she saw nothing. Assuming the Chief would be coming from town, she went back to the intersection and turned the other way, toward the dump exchange.

Just past the exchange, as she was scanning the trees, she noticed what appeared to be an old junkyard, littered with cars. It would be a great place to hide – or paint – a truck, she thought, and she turned around and drove back to the dirt road she thought might lead to the entrance. She dialed Joyce again, but the number was busy.

She turned onto the dirt road and crept slowly down its length, avoiding potholes as much as possible. A few yards in, there was a chain-link fence, and she followed it to a rudely constructed gate, where a makeshift sign read "Authorized Personnel Only -- Do Not Enter."

Gemma parked beside the gate and rolled down her window. Hearing nothing, she rolled it up again and stepped hesitantly out of the car. Looking both ways, she stepped past the sign and the fence and began walking down the narrow gravel lane that led to the cars she had seen from the road. Scattered among the trees were various species of what she had learned to call "island cars"

– mostly pickups, some 70's gas-guzzlers, and a number of sub-compacts, all badly rusted and missing doors, tires, and often windshields and roofs.

A few yards off, she heard an engine turn over, cough a few times, and roar to life, obviously lacking a muffler. She ducked behind one of the pickups just as a red VW bug sped by with Suzanne at the wheel. Gemma felt in her pocket for her cell phone, but she'd left it in her car. *Damn*, she thought – *I need to call the Chief. But where's Jasper? And what happened to the Snow Goose?*

Gemma was torn: it was possible Suzanne had abandoned the Snow Goose somewhere in the junkyard. Should she go back to her car and call the Chief? But what if Suzanne spotted her car parked by the entrance and was waiting for her?

The roar of the muffler had ceased. Was it because Suzanne had stopped to come back for her, or because she had driven unseeing by Gemma's car and was now on her way to the ferry dock? With a quick prayer for good luck, Gemma decided the most important thing was to track down the Snow Goose, and she headed deeper into the junkyard.

The day had started relatively clear, but a thick cloud cover had begun darkening the sky, bringing with it a cold drizzle. As Gemma headed deeper into the junkyard, the rain began in earnest. She pulled up her hood, but it didn't provide complete coverage, so her vision was blurred by the drops on her glasses. The dirt underfoot was fast becoming a slippery morass of mud, and it became increasingly difficult to watch where she was stepping.

Hearing a faint sound mixed in with the steady pelting of the rain on her hood, Gemma stopped to listen, but she could distinguish nothing beyond the rain and the cry of the crows feasting in the nearby apple orchard. Seeing a flutter of white in the distance, she headed in that direction, hoping it might be the Snow Goose.

As she drew closer, she could see that it was indeed a large white van, sandwiched between an elderly rusted pickup and a small bulldozer that was tipped on its side. Since she had never seen the Snow Goose, she couldn't be sure this was it, but there were windows along the side and it appeared to be in fairly good condition, so she drew closer, still listening for sounds above the noise of the rain and the crows.

Through one of the darkened windows of the van she caught a flash of movement. *Good,* she thought, *if the professor is trapped inside, he may still be alive*! Stealthily she moved around the back of the van to try the handle on the door. She had just begun to turn it when there was a sharp pain in the side of her head, the world went black, and Gemma slumped to the ground.

CHAPTER 39

"Interfering bitch," Suzanne snarled, and she threw the rock she had used to hit Gemma into the woods. She started back toward her car; there was still time to make the 11:45 ferry if she pushed it. About halfway down the road she found Jasper, sitting in the mud and sobbing. Apparently he had tried to follow her and had slipped.

"You fool," she said, picking him up and pushing him in front of her. "I told you to stay in the car."

"But where's Pastor Benson?" cried Jasper.

"She decided to pay the Professor a visit," snapped Suzanne. "I'm sure they'll be very happy together." She continued pushing and dragging the stumbling boy down the junkyard drive, and, opening the VW door, she shoved him into the back seat. "Now shut up," she said as Jasper continued crying. "I have enough on my mind without your whining."

Suzanne turned the key and the car roared to life and then died. She pumped the gas a few times, then tried again, and again it roared to life and then died. The gas gauge read full, so she tried one more time, and again it failed. She punched the guage and the needle dropped to zero.

"Shit," she swore, pounding the steering wheel. "Wait, maybe the bitch left the keys in her car," and she jumped out and headed for Gemma's car. It was unlocked, but when she opened the door the keys were not in the ignition or anywhere else she could see. Gemma's cellphone started ringing, and she slammed the door. "At least she didn't take that with her," she muttered. "That'll give me a little extra time."

Suzanne went back to her car and motioned angrily through the window to her son. "You stay put," she yelled, "I'll be right back," and she headed back into the junkyard. Surely the priest had her car keys with her; she'd just grab them and head out.

Jasper waited until his mom was out of sight, and then slowly opened the car door. Seeing nothing and no-one, he crept over to Gemma's car and opened the door. Gemma's cellphone was there on the seat; maybe he could use it to call for help. Can you dial 911 from a cellphone, he wondered? But just then the phone rang and vibrated, nearly jumping out of his hand. He opened it up and answered.

"Hello?"

"Jasper? Is that you?" It was Joyce's voice. "May I speak to Gemma?"

Jasper slid into the back seat of Gemma's car and ducked down on the floor, hoping his mom wouldn't come back and see him.

"I don't know where she is," whispered Jasper. "I'm just outside the junkyard, in her car," whispered Jasper.

"What's that?" asked Joyce. "You're breaking up; can you speak louder?"

"I'm at the junkyard in Gemma's car," shouted Jasper. "And my mom's done something bad to her and the professor; you need to get the Chief here right away!" Jasper hung up the phone, returned it to the front seat, and stumbled back to the back seat of the VW. He had just curled up there, pretending to be asleep, when his mom returned with Gemma's keys.

"Get out," said Suzanne.

"Wha...?" wailed Jasper, feigning sleep.

"Get out, dammit," repeated Suzanne. "Gemma gave me her keys so we can take her car. Let's go; we have a ferry to catch." Suzanne's long red hair was soaking wet and dripping into her eyes, and she was clearly very angry. Jasper decided it was probably foolish to stall any longer; hopefully the Chief had gotten his message and was on his way.

"Where's my stuff?" asked Jasper as he stumbled out of the VW. "Here," said his mom, handing him the bag from the hospital and reaching into the trunk for another just like it. Jasper looked in the bag she had given him to see if his pills were there, but – it was filled with money!

"This isn't my bag!" said Jasper. "Hey! This is that money from the barn?"

"Never you mind," said Suzanne, handing him the other bag. "Now give me that and get in the fucking car."

"No," said Jasper, "you can't make me. That money's for the Snow Goose!"

Jasper turned to run with the money but tripped in the mud and fell. The bag tipped and the money spilled out into the mud and rain as Jasper struggled to rise again. Suzanne threw his bag into Gemma's car and came after him. "Just stop it!" she shouted. "Get in the damn car and give me the fucking money." She grabbed Jasper just as he got to his feet, pulling him back down into the mud as she reached for the bills that had spilled out of the bag. Jasper twisted in her grasp, but she held him firm as she reached for the last two bills.

Grabbing the bag and Jasper, Suzanne rose to her feet just as a siren sounded in the distance. "Shit, what now?" she swore. "Get back in the VW," she said, tossing Gemma's keys onto the seat of the Subaru. "Now if they stop, shut up and let me handle this."

Suzanne tossed the money bag back into the trunk of the VW, slammed it shut, then got back into the driver's seat and pretended to try to start the car again. A police car drove up, blocked her way out, and the Chief got out of the car. He came over and knocked on Suzanne's window, which she obediently rolled down.

"What seems to be the problem, officer?" she asked, biting her lip.

"Seems we got a call there's a disturbance out here at the junkyard," said the Chief.

"Well, I'm certainly having a problem starting my car," said Suzanne. "Do you have some gas you could give me? It seems to be running empty and I have a ferry to catch."

"Do you now," said the Chief. "And who's this in the back seat? Is that you, Jasper?"

"Yes, sir," said Jasper, trying to make himself as small as possible.

"You're looking a little damp, boy," said the Chief. "Surely you haven't been out playing in the rain?"

"No, sir," said Jasper.

"You know how boys are," said Suzanne with a harsh laugh. "He was determined to go out; I had to come after him and now I'm stuck."

"I see," said the Chief, looking over the back seat. "Well, boy," he said. "I don't have any extra gas in my car, so I think you'll just have to get in my car and come with me. You got any dry clothes back here?" he said, opening the trunk. "Well!" he exclaimed, looking at the muddy bag with the wet money spilling over the edge. "What have we here?"

"What we have here," said Suzanne, springing from the car and pointing a gun at the Chief, "is a new life for me and my kid. So hand me the damn money and I'll be on my way," she added, waving the gun. "Don't make me use this; I just wanna get off this friggin' Rock."

The Chief put his hands up over his head. Inching backward he said, "I believe you'll have to get it yourself, ma'am. I'd never touch dirty money."

Still holding the gun on him, Suzanne stepped forward to grab the bag of money. At the same moment, Jasper threw open the back door of the VW, catching her in the side. Off balance, Suzanne staggered, slipped in the mud and fell against the Chief. The gun in her hand went off and Jasper cried out.

Chapter 40

"Mom, Mom," screamed Jasper, and he ran to Suzanne, who lay stunned in the mud.

"Out of the way, son," said the Chief, who had retrieved the gun and stood pointing it at Suzanne.

"Please don't shoot her," cried Jasper. "She wouldn't hurt anybody, really she wouldn't."

"Is that so, son?" said the Chief. "Then what would you call this?" Still holding the gun on Suzanne, the Chief rotated slightly on one hip and Jasper could see that his right pant leg was covered with blood.

"You're hurt," Jasper exclaimed, and turned to his mother. "Mommy, mommy, why did you hurt him? He was just trying to help us."

"Yeah, right," said Suzanne, pulling up to her elbows. "Help us. Like everybody else on this fuckin island tries to "help" us. By pullin' us down, holdin' us back, keepin' us stuck here. It's like a conspiracy, you know that?" she said, struggling awkwardly to her feet. "You come here, thinking it's gonna be different, you'll have a chance. But it's really just the same shit in a nicer place. Come on, Jasper, we're goin' home."

"I don't think so," said the Chief. "I believe you're going to the station; you've got some explaining to do." A siren sounded in the distance, and soon Pete pulled up in the other police cruiser.

"You okay, Chief? I heard the shot on your pager."

"Just a flesh wound," said the Chief. "Messy, though – and it hurts like hell."

"I'm calling the EMT's" said Pete, looking more closely at the Chief's leg. "This doesn't look good."

"Okay," said the Chief, "but first could you cuff this one?" he said, thrusting Suzanne toward Pete. "We need to get her down to the station. Jasper, if I carry you, do you think you can tell me where I'll find the Snow Goose?"

"You're not carrying anyone anywhere," said Pete as he snapped the cuffs on Suzanne's wrists. "You stay here with her and the kid, and I'll go see if I can find the van."

Pete went down into the junkyard and found Gemma lying outside the back of the distinctive white van. He radioed in to alert the medics that there were multiple wounded, then knelt down beside her.

"Pastor Benson, wake up," he said, checking her pulse. "Can you hear me?"

Gemma slowly opened her eyes and looked up at him. "Pete," she asked, rubbing her head, "Why did you hit me?"

"I didn't hit you," said Pete. "Suzanne did, and then tried to drive off with Jasper and the money."

"Is Jasper okay?" asked Gemma.

"He's fine, he's with the Chief now and Suzanne is handcuffed and lying in the back seat of my car," said Pete.

"Ow," said Gemma as the deputy helped her to sit up. "My head hurts like the dickens. And it's freezing out here."

"We've got an aid car coming," said Pete. "We'll get you warm and dry in no time. Now, where's the professor?"

"I think he may be locked up in the van," said Gemma. "I was trying to get him out when Suzanne hit me."

"Can you sit up by yourself?" asked Pete.

"I think so," replied Gemma. "Please, you've got to check on the professor."

Pete turned the handle of the van and opened the door. The professor was lying gagged and bound on the floor of the van, shivering. Pete removed the gag and began untying the ropes that bound him.

"Is he okay?" called Gemma.

"Pretty weak," said Pete. "How you doing, professor?"

"So cold," said the professor. "Wicked, wicked woman."

"Yes she was," said Pete. "No, don't try to sit up. You just lie there; the ambulance will be here any minute now; hear the siren? Here, I'll put my coat over you; maybe that will help. How long have you been in here?"

"Since last night," said the professor. "Has anyone checked on my dog?"

"Gunnar's fine," said Pete. "The Chief gave him some food this morning, and Joyce was planning to come by and walk him."

"Here, Pastor Benson, can you stand?" He helped her up. "You might be a little warmer sitting on the edge of the van; get you out of the rain. This may take a while – they also have to load the Chief into the ambulance."

"Oh, no, not the Chief!" said Gemma. "Is he okay?"

"Suzanne shot him. Just a flesh wound," he added, "but he's lost a fair amount of blood."

Gemma dropped her head into her hands and moaned. "Oh, my head."

"Hang in there," said Pete, wrapping his arm around her to keep her warm. "They'll be here any minute now."

Soon they heard the ambulance coming down the gravel drive. Pete left Gemma and the professor to go flag them down, and they pulled the ambulance around in front of the Snow Goose. The EMT's loaded Gemma and the professor into the ambulance with the Chief and Jasper, and the ambulance sped off to the clinic, sirens wailing, with Pete following close behind in the squad car.

CHAPTER 41

Later that afternoon Gemma stopped by the church to check in with Joyce.

"The responses are already coming in from the mailings," said Joyce. "And I hear you had an exciting morning!"

"Too exciting for me," said Gemma. "I'm going home; I plan to curl up in front of a warm fire in my jammies and just vedge out. Thanks for getting in touch with the Chief for me," she added.

"No problem," said Joyce. "All in the line of duty. And hey, you don't look so good," she added, looking more closely at Gemma. "Are you sure you shouldn't be at the clinic?"

"Been there, done that," said Gemma, "I'm fine, just a big lump on the back of my head. I can't wait to get home and take some Tylenol."

"Here," said Joyce, "I've got some in my desk. Why don't you sit down and have a cup of tea and get some meds before you head home: I'm not sure you're in any condition to drive."

Once Gemma had taken the meds and settled into the leather chair, her knees tucked up and her hands wrapped around a cup of tea, Joyce asked what she'd been dying to know. "So I gather you all ended up at the junkyard – what actually happened out there?"

"Well, as near as I can figure," said Gemma, "Suzanne had been shacking up with Drew Bailey. All those nights she claimed she was on the mainland for those massage classes she was actually coming home on the late boat and crawling in with Drew. Apparently they had to keep it quiet because Drew's divorce isn't final yet.

"And since Drew left his wife he's been staying in a cabin out at Bryce's place, so they used Bryce as their cover to keep Drew's wife out of the picture."

"Figures, said Joyce. "I never thought Bryce was actually into women that way. So what was she doing at the junkyard?"

"Well, it turns out Jasper *had* told someone about the money, just not directly. After he found it, he ran home with the two bills and he was all excited. As he was getting ready for bed that night, he mentioned to his mom that he'd found something really cool in the professor's barn that afternoon. He didn't tell her what it was, but, like most moms, she'd gotten in the habit of going through his pockets before throwing his clothes in the laundry. Seems she found the bills and decided not to say anything to Jasper.

"After Jasper went out the next morning – he was heading over to the church to put the money in the collection van – Suzanne went over to the barn, found the money, moved it out and covered over both their tracks: apparently Drew had been getting increasingly abusive, and she was planning to leave him and the island. The money was her ticket to freedom.

"When that bill turned up at the police station Monday morning, Drew realized it had to be from the stash from that U district heist that Hadley had hidden all those years ago. Turns out Hadley had been a student of the professor's, and had visited his island place from time to time.

"Drew thought the money had come from the Professor, so he went by his house pretending to be on police business. When the Professor mentioned that Jasper had had some trouble with Gunnar on Saturday, Drew, who knew Jasper had been sleeping at the church when his mom wasn't around, put two and two together.

"He went by the barn as soon as he could, but Suzanne had already cleared out the money. He assumed Jasper had taken it home, which was why he was looking in the house – and of course he knew where they lived because of his relationship with Suzanne."

"So how did the suitcase end up at the Exchange?"

"Suzanne didn't know that the police knew about Jasper's bills. All she knew was that the money was her chance to get away from Bailey and off the island. She didn't want the suitcase traced or identified, so she just dumped the money in a paper grocery sack and left the case at the exchange when no one was around."

"But why kidnap the professor?"

"Apparently when Suzanne was leaving the barn with the suitcase she saw the professor in the window at the house. When she came back later – having decided to just leave the suitcase back where she found it, she realized someone had been investigating the site. Not realizing it was Bailey, she assumed it was the professor, and worried he might spill the beans to the cops.

"She wanted to keep the professor quiet long enough to get off the island, and the simplest way was to take him with her to Anacortes, but she had to wait 'til Jasper was out of the Clinic because she couldn't leave him behind.

"She decided to pretend she was headed for the mainland so I would keep Jasper overnight, and then she doubled back to the professor's place. Once there, she knocked the professor out, trussed him up and gagged him and threw him into the van, and then left the van in the barn and drove home. The next morning she walked back to his house, leaving her car at her place so it would look like she had come back from the mainland, and she took the Snow Goose out to the Neck to pick up Jasper.

"When I found it so easy to follow her she realized the Goose was too easy to spot, so she dumped it at the junkyard and borrowed an old VW the island kids used to take on joyrides.

"Wow," said Joyce.

"Yeah," said Gemma. "But that's when I showed up. When she saw my car as she was leaving the junkyard in the VW, she figured I was poking around the junkyard and tracked me back to the Snow Goose just I was opening the van. She knocked me out and left me in the mud, but by then the Chief was onsite and the VW wouldn't start.

"She pulled a gun on him, but Jasper managed to slam into her with the car door; the gun went off when she fell and the Chief was hurt but he was able to subdue her anyway, and then Pete showed up. After that it was just a matter of getting us all to the clinic to deal with all the wounded!"

"So where's Suzanne now?" asked Joyce.

"They took her over to the county jail in Friday Harbor this afternoon. Apparently she and Drew are having a fine time hurling insults at each other from their adjacent cells." said Gemma.

"And the professor?"

"They're keeping him overnight at the clinic for observation," said Gemma. "He had hypothermia and was pretty dehydrated; when they pumped water into him had a mini heart attack so they're keeping a close eye on him. I think he'll be okay, but he is getting on in years; doesn't have the resilience of his younger days.

"I've sicced Eleanor on him," Gemma continued. "She's reading to him and playing chess and chuffing him a bit; seems she and her husband spent quite a bit of time with the Lindquists back in the day when her husband and Berit were still alive. I wouldn't be surprised if they start spending a lot more time together; she seems real comfortable with him," added Gemma.

"And the Chief?"

"He's fine, just a flesh wound; they got it cleaned up and sent him home. Jasper's gonna stay with him for a few days; they can convalesce together, take care of each other," she added.

"Those two, take care of each other?" snorted Joyce. "What the hell are they going to eat, takeout pizza? The Chief can't cook if he can't stand up."

"Well," said Gemma, "I did tell him I'd talk to you about maybe taking on the cooking chores 'til he gets back on his feet... I really want Jasper to stay there; I think he's very much in need of a father figure right about now. Plus he loves riding in the police car."

"Hmph," said Joyce. "Great. Like I don't have enough on my plate as it is. Oh, well. I was planning to make spaghetti tonight anyway; nothing says I can't make it at Jim's house as easy as I can make it at my own. Plus he's got a separate study; I could put Darla in there to do her homework after dinner while I do the dishes; I know those two are probably planning on watching the game on TV."

"Sounds like a plan to me," said Gemma. "Well, I'm gonna run on home. Give Jasper a hug for me; I'll stop by tomorrow, see how they're doing."

"Ok," said Joyce. "But be careful driving home. Call if you need anything. And by the way?"

"Yes?" said Gemma

"I have some news for you," said Joyce.

"What's up?"

"Marcia's husband has been diagnosed with liver cancer."

"Oh, I'm so sorry to hear that," said Gemma, turning back from the door. "What's his prognosis?"

"They're not sure yet," said Joyce, "but he'll be starting chemo on Monday."

"Oh, dear," said Gemma.

"So they've decided to put the house here on the market," said Joyce, "and they've rented a place in Anacortes so it will be easier for him to go to the hospital."

"Really!" said Gemma, sitting down. "That was fast!"

"Yes, well, turns out Marcia's been restless on the island for a while now; probably looking for a bigger pond. But you'll be happy to hear that George and Doris have agreed to take over the planning for the Christmas market," said Joyce, "...on one condition."

"What's that?" asked Gemma.

"George wants to have a barbecue instead of that spaghetti supper Marcia was planning," said Joyce.

"Really," said Gemma. "Interesting. Well. Um, I don't have a problem with that, do you?"

"Nope," said Joyce, grinning broadly.

Gemma looked around guiltily, then grinned back at Joyce. "Guess the Lord works in mysterious ways! Well, be sure you add Marcia and Orville to the prayer list," she added.

"Done," said Joyce. "And, oh, another thing. Harry came up with a fabulous fundraiser."

"Really," said Gemma.

"He thinks we should auction off all those cases of communion wine we have left down in the basement."

"Well that can't be worth much," said Gemma. "What sort of wine is it – and who would want 20 cases of communion wine?

"Oh, I should think we'll have folks beating down our door," said Joyce. "Turns out Father Parkinson was quite the connoisseur."

"Really," said Gemma.

"Mm-hmm," smiled Joyce. "Some of those bottles – and I'm not talking cases, I'm talking bottles – are worth over $80 apiece."

"Holy shit," said Gemma.

"Well, I don't think it's been blessed yet," said Joyce with a grin, "so it may not be holy shit. But it sure is expensive shit!"

"Wow," said Gemma, sitting down again. "And he paid for this – how?"

"I believe that was the evangelism budget," said Joyce. "That item comes out of a special endowment fund set up by young Elwood's wife," said Joyce.

"Really," said Gemma.

"But of course we could never talk about it under the terms of old Elwood's will, because evangelism and mission are forbidden topics," said Joyce. "It was always to be spent at the discretion of the priest."

"Curiouser and curiouser," said Gemma.

"I thought you'd be amused," said Joyce.

"Indeed," said Gemma, nodding her head. "Indeed."

"Well," she added, "on that note, I think I'll head home and fortify myself."

"Good idea. Want a bottle of communion wine to help with that?" she grinned broadly.

"Oh, God, no," snickered Gemma. "That's the last thing I need with this headache – and that bottle could be worth a new espresso machine for the church coffee hour! "Both women laughed at that. "So," she continued, pausing at the door, "we're all set for Sunday's service?" asked Gemma.

"Except for your sermon," said Joyce.

"Oh, great," said Gemma, "Thanks for reminding me – not!" She grinned back at Joyce as she headed out the door. "Wanna preach for me this Sunday?"

"In your dreams," said Joyce, shaking her head. "Can't wait to hear what you come up with!"

"Gee thanks," said Gemma. "And what did you say the lesson was again?"

"No problem," said Joyce. "I think it's that passage on money as the root of all evil."

"Wrong," replied Gemma. "It's not money, it's the *love* of money that's the root of all evil. Know your scriptures, child!" she grinned.

"No thanks," said Joyce. "That's your job – and see that you get it done by Sunday!"

"Ten-four, kiddo," said Gemma. "Have a good one!" and the exhausted interim priest for St.-Aidan's-by-the-Sea, Brandon's Rock, headed home.

CHAPTER 42

Dear Alex,

I'm sorry to hear you've been under the weather. Please take care of yourself, as I'd like you to be well in time for (dun, dun, dun) MY VISIT!!! I've decided I can't go a whole year without seeing you, and I've booked a ticket for Kerala. I'll be leaving after Christmas, as soon as Amy goes back to college, so expect me sometime around the 5th of January. I'll send details later.

Despite all the craziness of last week, Sunday's service went really well – we still opened with Rock of Ages (you have to keep some traditions alive), but the response to the new liturgy was good and Harry actually CHOSE to read the Message version of the Epistle. Chandler came up to me again after the service – apparently he fancies himself a composer – and he's offered to come up with some new service music for us; we'll see how that goes.

It's the first Sunday of Advent, by the way – I know there's a huge Christian population in Kerala, but I don't know if you've been going to church now that you don't have to… hint, hint. But it feels good. There's a real sense of hopefulness in the air here. I'm hoping you feel it, too…

Love,
Gemma
PS: See you soon!

G

APPENDIX A

Gemma's Bible Study : II Corinthians 9:6-15

After clearing her throat, Doris began reciting the following passage:

Remember that the person who plants few seeds will have a small crop; the one who plants many seeds will have a large crop. You should each give, then, as you have decided, not with regret or out of a sense of duty; for God loves the one who gives gladly. And God is able to give you more than you need, so that you will always have all you need for yourselves and more than enough for every good cause.

As the scripture says, "He gives generously to the needy; his kindness lasts forever." And God, who supplies seed for the sower and bread to eat, will also supply you with all the seed you need and will make it grow and produce a rich harvest from your generosity. He will always make you rich enough to be generous at all times, so that many will thank God for your gifts which they receive from us.

For this service you perform not only meets the needs of God's people, but also produces an outpouring of gratitude to God. And because of the proof which this service of yours brings, many will give glory to God for your loyalty to the gospel of Christ, which you profess, and for your generosity in sharing with them and everyone else. And so with deep affection they will pray for you because of the extraordinary grace God has shown you. Let us thank God for his priceless gift!

"Now then," said Gemma. "Did anyone find any significant differences in their translations? Harry? You're looking a bit puzzled; what did you find?"

"I'm reading the Revised Standard Version," said Harry. "And in that first section, where it said "you should each give?"

"Yes," said Gemma.

"My version just says each one must DO. So it isn't necessarily true that this passage is about giving."

"Good point, Harry. Anything else?"

"Well, where Doris said kindness, my Bible said righteousness. So the Good News Bible is making promises that God didn't necessarily say."

"Interesting," said Gemma.

"And in the last bit," added Harry, warming to his subject, "Doris said 'Many will give glory to God for your loyalty to the gospel,' but mine just says "you will glorify God by your obedience in acknowledging the Gospel." So Doris's bible says people will notice if you do what the gospel says, but mine just says it's the right thing to do."

"So Harry has brought us to an interesting point," said Gemma. "And one reason these two versions are so different is that Harry's version is an actual translation of the Bible from its original text, but Doris's Bible is what's known as an interpretation. Naturally any translation will reflect the bias of the translator to some extent, but an interpretation is more likely to be written with a specific intent on the part of the interpreter."

"Does anyone here have a King James Version? Ah, George. Did you notice any differences other than the obvious style of the language and the ones Harry has already raised? Because the King James Version, like Harry's, is actually a translation, not an interpretation."

"Actually," said George, "the King James says give in that first part, just like the Good News."

"Which makes sense," said Gemma, "because the Good News Interpretation is based on the King James translation."

"…but it, too, says righteousness instead of kindness," added George. "And the whole glorify thing is really confusing, and talks about subjection unto the Gospel."

"Ah," said Gemma. "So we begin to see why there was a need for new versions. Does anyone have the Message?"

"I do," piped up Flora.

"And how does that compare?" asked Gemma.

"It's really different; there don't seem to be any words in common with the others," said Flora.

"Do you think it means the same thing?"

"I'm not sure," said Flora. "But I like what it has to say."

GLOSSARY OF EPISCOPAL TERMS

Alb: White robe worn by many priests when celebrating communion, generally worn over daily clothes but under other vestments.

AA: Abbreviation for Alcoholics Anonymous, an alcoholism recovery support group which frequently meets in churches.

Acolyte: Lay volunteers, often youth, who follow the cross in the procession and recession and assist the priest in worship. An acolyte lights and sometimes carries candles, and sometimes helps in the preparation of communion.

Altar Guild: Special lay service group in a church who prepare the altar and maintain the furnishings in a church building. The altar guild usually supervises seasonal church decorations and flower arrangements.

Associate: Assistant clergyperson.

Benediction: Blessing at the close of a worship service.

Bishop: From the Greek word *episkopos*, meaning overseer. A bishop is a member of the highest of the orders of ministry in the Church.

Call: Assumed to be from God, the call suggests a particular ministry assignment.

Cassock: Black robe worn by priests or deacons, and are usually worn with a white over-garment called a *surplice*.

Cathedral: Church in which the diocesan bishop's throne or *cathedra* is kept; usually the largest parish in the Diocese.

Cathedral Day: Diocese-wide celebration of unity held annually at the Cathedral.

Celibate: Abstaining from sexual activity.

Censer: Vessel in which incense is burned on charcoal; usually carried in processions and recessionals by a special acolyte called a *thurifer*.

Chasuble: Type of vestment worn by the celebrant during Communion. It is usually oval in shape, with a hole for the head to pass through.

Cincture: Rope tied at the waist of a cassock.

Clergy: Group of ordained people consecrated for unique ministry for a particular church or denomination.

Communion: Christian sacramental meal, the Lord's Supper, now more commonly called the "Eucharist" in Episcopal churches. Also known as Mass in Roman Catholic churches.

Compline: Monastic evening service used to end the day, and included for the first time in the 1979 prayer book; pronounced "comp-lyn."

Diocese: Unit of church organization; the spiritual domain under a bishop. A diocese may contain many parishes and missions.

Epistle: A reading from one of the New Testament books other than the Gospels. The epistle and the Old Testament lessons are typically read by a lay reader.

Father: Familiar or direct way of referring to some ordained clergy.

Incense: Fragrant powder burned in a small dish or pot; used during the service or in the processions.

Interim: Clergy person appointed by the bishop after a priest leaves; assumes leadership of the church until a replacement priest is found.

Lay Reader: Any non-ordained person who participates in reading part of a church service.

Lectern:	A raised platform used for reading prayers or scripture; usually located at the front of the nave, opposite the pulpit.
Lectionary:	The complex series of Biblical readings used in the Episcopal Church throughout the year. The Church uses a three-year cycle of lessons for Sunday readings and a two-year cycle for daily readings.
Liturgy:	The complete worship service and how it is designed.
Mission:	Can refer to either a particular vision or outreach service or to a congregation which is not self-supporting and is therefore responsible to the bishop, meaning the priest-in-charge is a vicar rather than a rector.
Narthex:	An enclosed space at the entry end of the nave of a building; the area in the church building inside the doors and in front of the nave.
Nave:	The main part of a church building, where the congregation sits.
New Age:	Derogatory term used by traditional Christians to describe broader, more modern less Christ-based spiritual understandings.
Ordination:	The ritual used to make someone a priest or deacon, by the laying on of hands by a bishop.
Parish:	Established Episcopal congregation.
Parish List:	Membership roster.
Pastor:	Another name for a clergy person. In both Latin and English the word simply means "shepherd."
Popish:	Derogatory term used by low-church Episcopalians to refer to high-church activities that smack of Catholicism.
Prayerbook:	The worship book of the Anglican Church. Officially entitled "The Book of Common Prayer"

and commonly abbreviated as the BCP, the prayerbook is a collection of classic and contemporary prayers, services and psalms designed to allow the entire Church to worship in common union. The current prayerbook was last revised in the 1970's.

Priest:	Ordained minister of a Roman Catholic, Episcopal or Orthodox church.
Rector:	Head priest of a parish; the word, in Latin means "ruler."
Rite I:	Worship Service in the Book of Common Prayer which uses the traditional worship language of the Church as used from the 1600's until 1976.
Rite II:	Updated post-1976 Worship Service in the Book of Common Prayer which uses more modern language with a more egalitarian theological perspective than Rite I.
Sacristy:	Room near the altar where the communion vessels, altar hangings, candlesticks, vestments etc. are kept and cleaned. Used to be known as the Vestry.
Sanctuary:	The part of the church building behind the altar rail; sometimes used to refer to the whole inside of the church building.
Stewardship Campaign:	Annual drive, usually in November, to raise money for the church.
Stole:	Long strip of cloth (often silk) worn around the neck of the priest and allowed to hang down the front of the clerical vestments.
Vesting:	Donning vestments prior to a service.
Vestments:	Clothing worn by clergy or people leading a worship service.
Vestry:	Governing body of a church, made up of clergy, wardens, and lay members.

Vicar: Head priest of a mission, answers to the bishop.

Warden: One of two vestry members chosen to serve a parish in a special capacity. In many parishes the Senior Warden is chosen by the rector, and serves as a liaison between the rector and the parish, while the Junior Warden is elected by the parish at the annual congregational meeting and often runs the buildings and grounds committee.

White-knuckled
  Seminarian: Term used by Garrison Keillor to describe a recent seminary graduate who is anxious to share everything he/she knows about religion.

ABOUT THE AUTHOR

Diane Walker is a contemplative photographer and writer who has spent the last 20 years living on islands in the Pacific Northwest. After a career in hi-tech marketing she served as Communications Director for the Episcopal Diocese of Western Washington, as a licensed lay preacher, and on the faculty of the Diocesan School of Theology. A founding member of Good Samaritan, Sammamish, she sang in the choir, preached children's sermons, did terms as both Senior and Junior Warden, wrote the church song and designed the church logo. Now that her two beautiful daughters have grown and moved away, she lives with her husband, a goldfish, two cats and a blind, diabetic, coffee-loving dog on Bainbridge Island, where she enjoys acting, reading, painting, writing and photography and volunteers as exhibitions director of ECVA, a national artists registry with online exhibition space.

Diane offers a daily blog of photographs and meditations which can either be found on Facebook (search for Contemplative Photography by Diane Walker) or on the web at contemplativephotography.com. She has published three books of photographic meditations: *Illuminating the Mystery: Photographic Reflections on the Gospel of Thomas*; *From Loss to Love*; and *A Contemplative Photographer's Alphabet*, the last of which began as a traveling exhibit and has been displayed in several cathedrals across the US. She also provided the photographic illustrations for *Strength for the Journey: A Guide to Spiritual Practice*, by Renee Miller, and has lectured on Contemplative Photography as a Spiritual Practice in numerous venues.

Made in the USA
Monee, IL
20 May 2022